NIGHT STALKERS

A wide, flashing arc of five bullets split the night, and in its illumination Slocum saw the man he had hit . . .

The man's hands flew back, wanting to stem the flow of blood even as he was dead, drilled through the heart.

Slocum stood over the body, which twitched once and then was still.

It looked like one of Culhane's companions.

From above, Slocum heard a cry of anguish.

"Now, Slocum, you will pay with more than your life!"

JAKE LOGAN

SLOCUM AND THE INVADERS

BERKLEY BOOKS, NEW YORK

SLOCUM AND THE INVADERS

A Berkley Book / published by arrangement with
the author

PRINTING HISTORY
Berkley edition / April 1994

ISBN: 0-425-14182-9

BERKLEY®
Berkley Books are published by The Berkley Publishing Group,
200 Madison Avenue, New York, New York 10016.
BERKLEY and the "B" design
are trademarks belonging to Berkley Publishing Corporation.

PRINTED IN THE UNITED STATES OF AMERICA

10 9 8 7 6 5 4 3 2 1

1

Sometimes the night was friendly.

Sometimes it wasn't, of course. Sometimes it was deadly, with a full moon leaving you out in the open, in the hunter's sights, as plainly seen as if it were high noon. Sometimes the lack of moon was a deadly thing, a cautious night ride turned into death with a mount's slipped hoof tumbling its rider into a ravine, or down from a cliff's edge, to rocks and destruction far below.

Yes, the night was as capricious as the day. A sudden storm which might be seen a hundred miles away during daylight could creep over a night rider without warning and leave him open and unprotected. Slocum had once heard tell of a night tornado descending on a quiet Mexican town like a roaring train and wiping it from the face of the earth in a matter of minutes.

The night held at least as much danger as the day.

But it also held beauty. And this night, as he rode, Slocum was inclined to indulge in the beauty. The moon, a waxing slim crescent like a sickle

1

in the west, was a friendly orb tonight, as were the stars and the glowing band of the Milky Way, because there was no enemy at John Slocum's back and he was held in no hunter's cross hairs. Such had not been the case three weeks before, but three weeks could be an eternity to a man like John Slocum, who had indeed lived a life of eternities. Three weeks before he had been about as close as he'd ever been to death, even closer than when he had protested Quantrill's outrage at Lawrence, Kansas, so many years ago in the war, and had taken a bullet that nearly killed him . . .

Involuntarily, Slocum shuddered, thinking about the noose that had held his neck so tight just twenty-one days before, as well as the memory of those sights he had witnessed in Kansas during the War Between the States . . .

But the shudder was gone as quickly as it had come, and once again the night settled around Slocum, soothing him into a kind of peace.

Yes, the night could be kind, but even better than night and kindness was a half-full poke and a handful of Havanas.

Smiling to himself, Slocum pulled one of the slim cigars out, set it between his teeth and lit it up, scratching a lucifer to brilliance against his saddle. The smoke was fragrant and warming against the night chill. This might be Arizona in summer, but the desert nights still got cold, and fast, and any reminder of warmth was better than none.

Slocum's Appaloosa suddenly snorted, a sound that to Slocum's practiced ear meant that something lay in the night ahead.

Slocum immediately reined the horse in. He listened. Nothing, and then, yes, a sound, one that immediately stood up the hairs on the back of Slocum's neck.

The sound of metal against metal.

Possibly the sound of a weapon.

Slocum slipped from the Appaloosa's saddle soundlessly. Ahead he saw only brush and the flat of desert leading to some low hills.

The sound came again, and this time Slocum identified it as coming from the north.

A low hill stood against the near horizon.

And atop it was a figure, darkly outlined against the sinking Milky Way. Next to it was what looked like nothing less than a sniper's rifle on a tripod, pointed in Slocum's direction.

"Quiet, boy," Slocum whispered to his horse.

Pulling his Winchester from its scabbard, Slocum crept to the nearest stand of scrub and crouched behind it. Again the metallic sound came.

Slocum raised the rifle, sighted along it. An easy shot from this distance, especially to a sharpshooter.

The metallic sound came again, and along with it the word "Heavens!" in a man's voice.

Then Slocum heard another voice, decidedly feminine.

Stepping sideways, he moved closer, to the next stand of low brush. He repeated the process, now lying no more than twenty feet from the couple.

"Heavens!" the man's voice cried again, and the female voice answered, "Oh, Professor, here it is!"

"Capital!" the man's voice cried. He turned to the rifle-looking object, and once again there was the sound of metal against metal.

Slocum stood up, rifle at the ready, and said, "You shouldn't go pointing things at strangers, mister."

"Lord!" the man beside the rifle-looking object said, and Slocum tensed as something small and metallic flew from the man's hand to land in the darkness.

"Oh, dear!" the man said, advancing toward Slocum.

"That's far enough, mister," Slocum said.

The man, now a mere five feet away, stood up and blinked at Slocum in the near-darkness.

"What?"

"My goodness, he has a gun!" the female voice said.

Keeping the rifle on the man, Slocum turned his gaze to the woman, who now stood regarding him with fiery eyes.

"I'll bet he's a bandit, Professor!" she said, a look of repulsion, fear and anger crossing her features. "I'll bet he's going to rob us!"

The professor continued to blink, uncomprehending.

Slocum said, indicating the instrument on the tripod with the tip of his rifle, "I only aim a weapon at those who aim one at me."

"What!" the professor cried.

The girl suddenly began to laugh.

"Professor," she said, "he thinks your telescope is a *weapon*!"

"Preposterous!" the professor cried. He bent to retrieve the metallic object that had fallen to the ground, backed toward the tripod and fit the object into the far end of the tube.

"Absolutely preposterous . . . ," the professor mumbled.

Putting his hand on the long tube of the instrument, he swung it suddenly toward Slocum, who tensed.

"I'd get that thing away from me, if I were you," Slocum said.

The girl continued to laugh, and Slocum now noticed out of the corner of his eye that she was a pretty thing indeed, with a nice laugh to go with her fiery eyes.

"But—" the professor said, pointing out beyond where Slocum stood.

"I said get it away!" Slocum warned.

"Very well!" the professor said glumly. "But I'm telling you we only have a few more minutes to view Omega Centauri, and then it will be gone!"

The girl, laughing, pointed over Slocum's shoulder.

Slowly, still ready to fire if needs be, Slocum turned to see a fuzzy blot of light near the western horizon.

"That?" he said.

"Out of the way!" the professor said.

The girl was suddenly at Slocum's side, and took his arm.

"Come with me," she said, leading him to the telescope, smiling all the way, her fiery eyes empty of fear now but still filled with life.

2

When Slocum looked into the eyepiece of the telescope, he thought a magical trick had been played on him for sure. He'd seen such con men before, in St. Louis and in California; they set up a gizmo, a large box with doo-dads attached to it that supposedly played poker or chess, but there was always a flimflam involved. Once Slocum had seen a very angry and very drunk card player draw a gun on a box and start firing; only the quickness of the little fellow who'd been packed inside had saved his hide, as he started shouting and banged his way out of the box.

Slocum brought his eye away from the eyepiece, looked again at the fuzzy patch of light, then looked back into the instrument to behold an explosion of stars bursting out from a warmly glowing core of magnificent light, to spread in little pinpoints to the very edges of his vision.

"It's a trick," Slocum said, stepping away.

"Oh, foolishness!" the professor said, pushing Slocum out of the way impatiently. A moment later he sighed with disappointment and drew away from the telescope.

"It's gone," he said.

Slocum looked to see that the fuzzy patch of light had, indeed, dropped below the horizon.

"Do you believe it's not a weapon now?" the girl asked, the corners of her mouth still turned up in amusement.

"Indeed not," the professor said. "It's an Alvan Clark refracting telescope with an objective of six inches, manufactured to my specifications!"

The girl nodded.

"I still say it's a trick," Slocum said.

"Anything but," the professor replied. "The light entering the objective lens is merely magnified into the ocular lens at the opposite end." He drew the small metal tube that Slocum had looked into out of its slide. "The power of the telescope can be altered by replacing these oculars." He reached into his pocket and produced another.

"Watch," he said.

He swung the barrel of the telescope around, nearly hitting Slocum in the head. Again the girl laughed. This time the professor trained the instrument on the moon. Once he had it set up, he said to Slocum, "Look."

Slocum looked through the ocular, and now he was sure he was being tricked. The sliver of moon he could see was covered with pockmarks, mountains, plains and shadows, as if it were just down the road.

Slocum left the eyepiece behind, went to the

other end of the barrel and looked into the large flat glass mounted there.

"So where is it?" he said.

"Where is what?" the professor said.

"The trick?"

The professor cried out in anguish. "I told you—!"

Again the girl was at Slocum's side, taking his arm and leading him back to the eyepiece.

"There's no trick," she said. She kept her hand on his arm longer than she should have. Her smile was briefly inviting. "Look again."

Slocum fixed her with his gaze.

"I'd like to."

In the moonlight, he was sure she blushed.

"Just look at the moon—for now," she said.

3

After an hour Slocum was just about convinced he wasn't being tricked. The professor showed him wonderful sights—galaxies that looked like whirlpools of light, something else that looked like a smoke ring in the night, stars that split in two when the professor put a higher powered eyepiece in the instrument. There was even a comet visible, something Slocum remembered vaguely reading about a few years before, when all the papers had talked about the one that visited earth in 1886. At the very least, it was a good act.

"So where you two figure to set up your show?" Slocum asked.

The professor looked at him with puzzlement.

"Show?"

"Your tent. You have a tent, or you fixin' to hook up with a traveling show? There's a couple fellows out in California who'd love to have you along. Who knows, there may be a show in Flagstaff at the moment. That's only a day's ride away. You could make a good living I imagine."

"I don't understand . . . ," the professor said.

10

"Don't you figure on making some gold with this equipment?" Slocum asked.

Again the girl broke into laughter.

"The professor is quite wealthy!" she said.

"That's true . . . ," the professor said. "I have no need for money, and certainly would never use this instrument for that purpose."

"Then what good is it?" Slocum asked.

The professor looked as if the thought had never occurred to him.

"Why, it's—"

Suddenly he looked beyond Slocum and pointed.

"Look! Myra, it's up!"

Huffing with excitement, the professor fumbled with his telescope, turning it toward the eastern horizon.

Ignoring these antics, Slocum sidled up to the young woman, who now bustled about with energy, arranging a tray of eyepieces on a small table.

"So, your name's Myra, is it?" Slocum asked.

"Later!" Myra said, ignoring him. "Don't you see it's come up?"

Slocum turned to see what all the fuss was about, and beheld nothing more than a small reddish dot hanging now above the east.

"So?"

"It's Mars!" the professor shouted excitedly, adjusting the focusing knob on his instrument. "The planet Mars! And it's nearly at opposition now! Perfect for study!"

Scratching his head, Slocum began to walk away, back toward his mount.

"Screwy," he said to himself. "Has a shell game but doesn't want to play it, and now he's loco over a red dot in the sky."

"Where are you going?" Myra called out after him.

"Sorry, ma'am, it's time for me to move on. This just isn't my type of setup."

"But you must help us!"

In the barely lit darkness, she ran after him, caught up just as Slocum was hauling himself up into his saddle.

"Can't I persuade you to stay?" she said, staring up at him with her fiery eyes.

"Well, ma'am, that might just be possible . . ." Slocum shook his head. "Sorry. Just a little too out of bounds for me."

"We need a guide," Myra said. "And I need . . ."

She flashed her eyes, and a hint of a smile.

Slocum sighed.

"I'm tempted, ma'am. But—"

At that moment a shot split the night, and Slocum's mind was made up for him.

4

Automatically, Slocum threw himself from his Appaloosa and dropped to the ground, taking Myra with him. Still bearing his Winchester, he shielded the young woman, his senses suddenly keen and alive, and tried to determine where the shot had come from and to not give the shooter a target.

"Professor!" Slocum called out curtly. "Are you all right?"

"Quite!" the professor called out, and now Slocum located him, wisely on the ground next to his instrument.

Another shot pierced the air, hitting near the telescope's tripod.

"Oh, dear, they'll destroy my instrument!"

"Just stay down and stay quiet!" Slocum ordered.

When a third shot rang out, Slocum's senses were ready. The shot had come from a small rise back beyond them all a couple of hundred feet.

"Don't move," Slocum whispered to Myra, who nodded, looking at him with sudden fear.

Stealthily, Slocum inched away from the woman and angled himself around on the desert floor to take aim at the spot where the last shot had originated.

When another muzzle flash came, Slocum pulled off two rifle shots, and grunted with satisfaction when he heard a cry of pain.

"Did you get him?" Myra said.

"Could be—"

And then Slocum saw a figure rise from the desert and hobble in the near darkness to a waiting horse.

"Damn," Slocum cursed, rising up and jumping onto his own mount, but already he knew it was too late.

"Don't leave us!" Myra shouted.

"Be right back," Slocum called as he wheeled around to chase the already fleeing shooter.

When he reached the spot where the shots had come from, he pulled up and dismounted. Already, in the distance, the shooter was pulling away, nothing more than a dark blur of flight.

Slocum studied the area and found two spent shells, which he pocketed. Overhead the sky was beginning the lighten with coming daybreak, and the sinking Milky Way and moon no longer gave light to the darkness.

Slocum found the growing light helpful, however, and soon located a patch of blood on the sand where the shooter had lain. Beside it was a bandanna, the sight of which made Slocum curse.

"Thought I'd ridden away from that," he muttered to himself.

He thrust the bandanna into his pocket, mounted his Appaloosa, and wheeled back to the spot where Myra still lay.

In the coming light she looked even more fetching, and Slocum had an idea that in daylight she would be quite a sight indeed.

Myra rose and dusted herself off as once again Slocum dismounted, leaving his Appaloosa to walk back with the young woman to where the professor was once more staring with rapture through his eyepiece at the tiny red dot now climbing overhead.

"Syrtis Major! I've spotted Syrtis Major!" he shouted as they approached. "The seeing in this vicinity is excellent!"

"I'm afraid that—"

"I know, I know! Sunrise is coming! If only I had another two hours! My sketchbook, quickly!"

Myra scurried away to retrieve his sketchbook, which lay on a shelf under the table bearing the eyepieces, and handed it to the professor, along with a thin, dark pencil.

"And the polar cap! Excellent!" the professor cried.

Slocum, preoccupied with the sight of the bandanna, which he now pulled from his pocket to examine again, watched as the professor began to sketch in his book almost without taking his eye from the telescope; again, what Slocum saw on the page, a huge orb crisscrossed with lines and channels, he thought could not possibly have anything to do with the tiny dot the professor was studying through the instrument.

"Another trick?" Slocum asked.

"Hardly!" the professor cried impatiently. "Here, look, before it's too late!"

The professor moved reluctantly away from the instrument, still sketching in his pad, and Slocum took his place at the eyepiece.

What he saw again convinced him that he was being snookered—a foggy globe which came and went in focus, topped with a snowy white cap and covered with misty patches of reddish shadow which somehow resembled the professor's drawing—

"Out of the way!" the professor said, elbowing Slocum aside, and now, as the sun began to peek over the east, the professor made a last speedy effort to complete his drawing, which he did with a flourish.

"There!"

When he left the eyepiece, dawn was breaking, and Slocum could no longer make out the ruddy red dot overhead.

The professor, who, now that Slocum was able to study him in the light, revealed himself as a tall, thin gentleman with trim mustaches, thinning hair and an aristocratic bearing, sighed, looking up at the sky, and said, "Until tonight, then!"

Slocum turned to study Myra, who he now saw was studying him just as intently. She was indeed a fetching sight in daylight, with cascades of reddish hair and her flashing eyes a shade of green that Slocum had never before seen.

Her smile was as fanciful as her flashing eyes.

"Yes," she said, leveling her gaze on Slocum. "Until tonight, then."

5

It was only after Slocum had helped the professor and Myra break camp that he brought up the matter of the bandanna. There wasn't much of a camp to break; the professor and Myra had a single wagon drawn by two pack mules, filled mostly with equipment and a few days' worth of foodstuffs.

"How long did you expect to live out here?" Slocum asked, surprised at the meagerness of their stores.

Myra answered, "Two days. The professor heard that this spot had good seeing, and we only came out to test it. We'll be back in Flagstaff tomorrow, and then head out to other sights from there."

Slocum said, "Sounds a little foolish to me—"

Myra took his arm and led him out of earshot of the professor.

"That's what I've been telling him!" she whispered fiercely. "But he won't listen! There are Indian raiding parties out here, and bandits, but he thinks this is as civilized as Boston!"

"It's not, ma'am, believe me."

18

"Then tell him! He won't listen to me, and I'm afraid something will happen—"

For the first time since Slocum had met her the night before, he saw her fierce exterior broken. She leaned against him, trembling.

"What exactly does he have in mind?" Slocum asked.

"He wants to build an observatory out here, in the Arizona Territory, to look at Mars!"

Slocum almost laughed. "He wants to build *what*?"

"A huge telescope, under a dome! It's his dream!"

"So that's it? He *is* cracked, just like I thought."

"No! He's a brilliant man, and already famous!" Suddenly she drew away from Slocum. "And it occurs to me, now in the daylight, that I don't even know your name, or who you are!"

Slocum smiled wryly and bowed.

"John Slocum, at your service."

Suddenly demur, she said, bowing her head, "And my name is Myra Hendricks, of Boston, Massachussets."

"Ah," Slocum said, barely able to keep from laughing. "And last night you were?"

Myra blushed. "Last night I was frightened. And . . ." She gave him a slight smile. "And feeling very alone."

"I see."

She clutched at him, and again showed fear. "And I'm asking you again to help us!"

Slocum scratched his chin. "Well, now, like I said—"

"There's fifty dollars gold in it for you, for a week's work. All you have to do is . . . be with us. Protect us."

"Fifty?" Slocum said, indredulously.

"It's not enough? Seventy-five, then."

"That's more than enough, ma'am," Slocum said. "But—"

"What is it, then?" She leaned into him, and Slocum felt her warmth. "I can promise you, Mr. Slocum, that I very often get afraid at night, and feel alone."

Slocum looked down into her green eyes, and thought he could lose himself in them.

"Unless of course you're not interested," she purred.

"It's not that at all. It's just that I was planning on moving on. And . . ."

"And?"

Slocum nodded his head at the professor. "Your stargazer there makes me nervous. Trouble seems to get attracted to crackpots like that." Slocum thought of the rider who had shot at them the night before. "And I've already got enough trouble following me, and believe me, you don't need any of that."

"We'll take our chances." Her eyes were begging him, and, without his noticing, she had slipped her hand down behind his belt and was expertly fondling him to quick hardness.

"Please, Mr. Slocum," she purred. "For me."

To his rigid surprise, Slocum found himself nodding yes, just as her soft, long fingers found the root of his love shaft, then climbed subtly up to grasp his head and cover it, just as his cum load shot forth, making both he and Myra gasp in pleasure.

She removed her wet hand from behind his belt, still gazing up at him with her blazing green eyes.

"Thank you, Mr. Slocum."

"You're welcome, ma'am." Slocum said, smiling to himself.

"Call me Myra," she said.

"Myra, then," Slocum answered. "As long as you know what you're getting into."

"As long as *you* do, Mr. Slocum," she said, and they both laughed.

6

After breakfast they went their separate ways. The professor and Myra, their wagon loaded, headed off to scout a new sight for that night's telescope test, and Slocum rode off for a while in search of clues as to the whereabouts of the rider who had shot at them the night before. He knew the man wouldn't be too far off, just as he knew with near certainty who the man was. He was still angry that this trouble had followed him.

"I'll meet up with you well before sundown," Slocum said as they all headed out. "Listen to me, and there'll be no trouble. Stay out in the open as much as you can; this way you'll see anyone coming from miles off. And whatever you do, don't set up that tripod until I get back. Anyone is liable to think it's a weapon, like I did."

The professor nodded. "Very well, Mr. Slocum. And thank you for agreeing to stay with us. I'm sure it makes Myra here feel much safer."

Slocum and Myra exchanged glances, and subtle smiles.

"I'm sure it does," Myra said.

Slocum felt a slight pang of guilt as the wagon drew off, but this was quickly overtaken by the fact that if he didn't do something about the rider who had stalked him, they would all be worse off in the end.

His hope only turned to frustration as the day wore on, however. The bandanna remained his only clue. The man had done a good job of covering his tracks, as Slocum had been afraid he would, and all Slocum had after hours of riding was a certainty in his gut that the man would be back on his own terms, and possibly with help.

It had been a bad business all around, and once again Slocum found himself rubbing at his neck where that noose had been tightened, and momentarily shuddering.

The face of the man who had worn the bandanna—the hard eyes, the beard stubble, the set mouth of a killer, the knife scar high on the forehead that the bandanna never fully covered—rose up in front of Slocum again. How could it not, since this was the man who had tightened that noose, the hard eyes never leaving Slocum's, as the man had decided that it was time for John Slocum to die, and that he, Vern Culhane, should be judge, jury and executioner. And it was the *enjoyment* in the back of those hard eyes that had gotten to Slocum. Slocum had met many hard men, and cruel men, but somehow Culhane had been different. He was something worse than a man. Even Quantrill had been human, in some sense of the word. Horribly flawed, yes, but still a man. But Vern Culhane . . .

Slocum should have know that a man like Culhane would never give up—that his desire for Slocum's death would never leave until that noose had not only tightened but done its job . . .

Another slight shudder went through Slocum. It had been like looking into the eyes of an alien being.

Like another life form, or human form but not human. Something that not only enjoyed human suffering but *needed* it, like nourishment.

A monster.

Again Slocum shuddered. Not something he had often done.

But then iron resolve filled him, and he knew he would do what had to be done.

He only regretted having brought Myra and the professor into the mess.

But that, too, was done, and Slocum would honor his word and do what he could for them. In many ways they were better off with him around, even with the trouble following him.

And then, of course, there were those strange green eyes of Myra's, and that seductive smile . . .

Slocum found himself riding just a little easier, his problems pushed aside until he needed them, the memory of those flashing green eyes making the ride almost a pleasant one.

7

When Slocum rode up within sight of the wagon, well before sundown, he thought at first he had made a bad mistake in leaving them alone. The professor and Myra were nowhere in sight, and there, on a rise, in plain sight from a mile away, was the tripod and telescope Slocum had told them not to set up.

The mules hadn't bolted, which meant there probably hadn't been gunplay. Nevertheless . . .

Slocum approached carefully, Winchester ready across his lap. He circled the area, looking for signs of the duo but finding none.

Finally he approached the campsite head-on, dismounting fifty yards away with rifle at the ready.

A crude top had been erected over the wagon. Slocum saw the remains of a meal, a coffeepot still steaming, dishes neatly stacked off to one side.

The professor's notebook and eyepiece case were opened neatly on their table next to the telescope.

Slocum turned his attention to the wagon.

He feared what he might find inside. What if he had been wrong? What if indeed a rogue Navajo raiding party had found them, sneaked up stealthily and murdered them? What if Culhane had doubled back and come across them? Or any of a hundred other bandits, madmen or just plain killers?

Slocum lifted the flap of the cover on the wagon with the tip of his Winchester, and for a moment his heart sank.

There inside were the unmoving forms of the professor and Myra, apart, covered with a light blanket up to their faces, looking for all the world as if death had claimed them.

Slocum could not tell if they had been scalped, but—

Then the professor snored and turned over.

Myra opened her green eyes and sat up to stare at Slocum.

She smiled.

"What the—" Slocum said.

Myra looked past Slocum at the lowering sun. She gently reached over to shake the snoring professor.

"Professor, time to get up!"

"Sleeping?" Slocum said.

"Of course!" Myra said, climbing from the wagon and stretching. "All astronomers sleep during the day and stay up all night! Didn't you sleep today at all?"

Almost with embarrassment, Slocum realized that he hadn't. The matter of Vern Culhane had been so prominent on his mind that, as so often happened, sleep had merely been pushed to the side.

"My goodness, if you don't at least nap, you'll never be able to observe with us tonight!"

The professor had awakened, and now drew himself from the wagon. He, too, stretched, and immediately looked at the sky.

"Looks like it will be an excellent night for observing!" he said.

"Yes!" Myra chirped in.

"Are you both loco?" Slocum said. "How long have you been asleep?"

The professor studied the lowering sun. "Six hours at least. We found this spot before noon. Although I really think we'll have to get higher, into the mountains closer to Flagstaff, for the absolute best spot. There are hazes down here that tend to collect. Up in the mountains we'll get above all that, as well as above some cloud cover. I thought as much from the beginning— but at least we will have a good night tonight!"

Slocum shook his head. "Truly loco."

The professor looked apologetic.

"I'm sorry about not heeding your advice about setting up the tripod, Mr. Slocum, but it really could not be avoided. I'm afraid there would not have been enough time before dark. There were adjustments that had to be made, in order to make use of the equatorial mount. This allows us to follow the turning of the stars overhead easily, of course, and you must realize—"

Slocum, still shaking his head, began to walk away.

"Loco, plain loco. I should have left last night . . ."

Myra caught up with him.

"You can't go!"

"Watch me," Slocum said, filled with anger. "I tell you the simplest things to do, and you don't listen! I can't work like that!"

He kept walking away.

"But that man was near here—wearing a bandanna like the one you found last night!"

Slocum stopped dead in his tracks.

"When?"

Myra said, "This afternoon, while we were setting up the telescope. He was about a mile away, on horseback. The professor turned the telescope his way and got a good look at him before he turned and rode off."

Slocum turned to the professor.

"What did he look like?"

"Well, I did get rather a clear look at him for a moment. Rather grizzled looking. I actually was able to see a scar above his eyes—"

"Vern Culhane. Definitely," Slocum said.

"So you know this man?" Myra said.

"Yes."

"You won't leave now, will you?"

Slocum sighed and walked back to the campsite, Myra following.

"No. It would be murder if I did." He snorted. "It was probably your telescope there that saved your lives."

"You see?" the professor said. "It was wise to set it up after all."

Slocum grunted. "I suppose so."

Myra got Slocum a cup of coffee and gave it to him. "Are you hungry?"

"Well, as a matter of fact I am."

"Good. Then eat," Myra said.

In a few minutes she had prepared him a meal of cold beans and biscuits. "I'd heat them, but the fire went out at midday, and the professor wouldn't want the smoke now. It could harm the lenses."

"Sure," Slocum said, still amazed at the antics of these two.

Myra came to sit by him, while the professor began to putter around his instrument.

"And then you should get a couple of hours' sleep yourself, so that you can stay up the night with us," she said.

"Yes, you should," the professor said.

"You're right about that," Slocum said. "If Vern Culhane was going to try anything, he'd wait till dark." Slocum turned his attention to the professor. "There's something I'd like to get straight," he said.

"Hmmm?" the professor said distractedly.

"Myra here said something about seventy-five in gold if I trail along with you two for a week or so. Is that agreeable to you?"

The professor, eye glued to the eyepiece, waved his hand.

"Whatever Myra says is fine, my good fellow. She handles all of those things for me."

"Well, all right," Slocum said. "Then I guess we've got a deal."

Myra reached out and squeezed his arm.

"Good," she said, smiling.

Slocum shook his head.

"Though I sure still don't know what I've gotten myself into."

"Nothing you can't handle," Myra answered, still smiling.

8

Slocum was brought out of sleep by what he thought was someone reaching for the Colt in his cross-draw holster. He bolted awake, but before he could make a move, he relaxed to see Myra Hendricks leaning over him, smiling, her hand once again snaking its way behind his belt.

"Time to get up," she said.

"There's only one right way to do that," Slocum said.

In a moment he had pulled her down on top of him and rolled over.

"Time for me to use *my* hands," he said.

In a moment they had half their clothes off, then Myra tensed.

"The professor—" she said.

"Good thing I chose this spot away from camp," Slocum said, after glancing at the professor puttering around his instruments a good thirty yards away in the darkness.

Myra smiled up at him.

"Yes, it is," she said, and before long the other half of their clothing was gone.

31

Myra pressed herself up at him, moaning softly, and before Slocum had even gotten a taste
of her erect nipples, she had curled around his
hardened member and drawn him deep into her
wet recesses.

"You don't waste time, do you?" Slocum
panted.

"Not when there's not a lot of time," Myra
moaned, moving under him until he was even
deeper.

Slocum went to work, driving in and then
almost pulling out before driving home again.
Myra's moans began to build. She was tight but
lubricated inside, a perfect love machine, and
Slocum found himself marveling at her perfect
body, breasts standing out like red-tipped cones,
belly flat as a board.

"Let it go now!" Myra huffed fiercely, and Slocum
found himself willing to oblige, his cock swelling
with readiness.

"Yes!" Myra commanded, and at that moment
Slocum let her have what she wanted, driving high
and deep as his sex gun fired a mighty blast inside
her. He thought she would explode, her mouth
opening wide in a silent scream of pleasure, her
green eyes growing huge and even more fiery as
she clutched his buttocks, clawing into him with
each shot of his cum machine.

And then suddenly in the middle of it she fired off
her own volley, her body tightening like a spring,
arching, her nether triangle heaving, rivers of fluid

riding up and down around Slocum's shaft, driving him to even more orgasm, a final mighty burst of white love juice that drove her back on the ground, making her pull her hands from him to cover her mouth and keep from screaming out in ecstacy.

Suddenly, they both collapsed, the deed done, panting in each other's arms.

"I've never felt like that before, John Slocum," Myra gasped, trying to catch her breath. "Where I come from they don't . . . cum like that."

Slocum saw her smiling at her own pun.

"In Boston?" Slocum asked.

The focus seemed to come back to her fiery eyes. "Where?"

"You just said where you come from—"

"Yes! Boston, of course!" Myra said, quickly.

Slocum looked at her, but she just pulled away from him, letting him admire her perfect body as she dressed.

"The professor will need me," she said, but before she hurried off, leaving Slocum to dress and get ready for the night, she stopped to kiss him quickly.

"Where I come from, they don't . . . ," she said mysteriously, and then she was gone.

9

And then, with pleasure over, it was time to work.

Before joining Myra and the professor in the camp, Slocum made a wide, slow turn around the perimeter, Winchester at the ready. He saw now that the spot the professor had chosen wasn't so bad, especially at night. Their small rise sloped down to all compass points, and, with the clear sky, fattening moon and the glowing band of the Milky Way already rising in the east, he would be able to see any intruder a good mile off. There was little cover out there, too, which made Slocum's mind even easier.

As he walked, he tried to think what Vern Culhane might have in mind. If he were Culhane, he'd go back and get help, return with his three men. But that would take time. But perhaps Culhane had already brought his gang with him, and they were only a short ride away. That seemed more likely. In that case Slocum had to be ready at all times. Culhane's henchmen were nearly as ruthless as he was.

34

And a strange lot they were, too. In all his years Slocum had never seen a group quite like them. In many ways their tightness reminded him of Quantrill and his men. More a band of cutthroat pirates than anything, a club of murderers held together by their common bloodthirstiness.

But this group was cold as snow. Slocum, in the two days he had been involved with them, had never seen either Culhane or one of his boys crack a genuine smile, or make a joke that wasn't cruel. All business. That alone should have clued Slocum as to their intentions toward him. Had he known how they'd butchered those two miners just a day before he hooked up with them, he would have shot it out with them right then and there. The miners had been cut up like cattle, Slocum had heard later, after he'd gotten away.

Again he felt the noose mark around his neck.

Cold. Cold like ice they'd been.

Prospectors he'd known they weren't. Though that's what they'd said they were. After all, how many men were involved in rustling minerals? It just didn't make sense. And they were looking for a particular ore, one that Slocum had never even heard of. They'd know it when they saw it, that was the way Culhane put it.

So, having little else to do, and out of boredom, Slocum had hooked up with them, suppressing the bad signs. A couple days' work, helping them check out abandoned mine shafts, and then a good payoff in gold.

Culhane had even showed him the gold haul they had. And the way Culhane had acted, it was as if the gold meant nothing to them. A sack of tiny ingots; Slocum had even found a couple on the ground, carelessly left by one of Culhane's men after breaking camp.

They had gold, and plenty of it—so even if they were cold customers, could it hurt to go along with their craziness and take some of that gold off their hands?

It had been the deadliest decision of Slocum's life.

They searched abandoned mines, using maps they had. And Culhane and his bunch had only grown angrier and angrier at each site, when not a sign of what they wanted was found.

"You're holding out on us," Culhane had said, confronting Slocum on the second day.

Still, Slocum had not seen the viciousness coming. He'd merely shrugged and said, "Can't give you what you want when it's not there, can I?"

"You've got twelve more hours, Slocum," Culhane had said, turning those frigid eyes on Slocum before walking away.

Slocum had merely laughed to himself, figuring the man was loco.

But then, that night, after searching yet another futile abandoned mine, Slocum had begun to think that maybe loco was more than he could handle. He had seen the way Culhane acted in the mine. When they'd come up empty-handed,

Culhane had pulled the rafters down behind them as they left, collapsing the shaft in rage. Slocum had never seen such raw anger in his life, not even in Quantrill.

"Tomorrow morning, Slocum," Culhane said as they bedded down for the night.

But Slocum had decided not to be around for the morning. So when the others had gone to sleep, he packed his bedroll and supplies onto his Appaloosa and prepared to ride out.

"Going somewhere?" Culhane said, seeming to appear from nowhere behind him. At his side were two of his three men, pistols drawn.

"Yes I am, Vern," Slocum said, trying to stay reasonable. At the same time his hand was ready to go for his Colt. "I think what I'm going to do is ride out tonight. You don't owe me a thing. The only gold I'm taking is what I found on the ground after we broke camp yesterday. Your men left it behind, and I figure it's finders keepers. I don't want anything else from you."

"But I want plenty more from you," Culhane said. "You agreed to stay on till we found what we want."

"Whatever that is," Slocum answered, his voice hard. Then, thinking it prudent, he softened his tone.

"Look, I just want out. You boys can find what you want on your own. You know how to search a mine. Just keep doing what you're doing and you'll find what you want straight off."

"We want you along for the ride, Slocum."

Slocum hardened his voice again.

"Like I said, I want out."

And that was the last thing he said. Culhane's other man came up from behind and cold cocked him with a gun butt.

And when he awakened, he was being strung up from a tilted timber at the mouth of the mine shaft they'd last searched, sitting on his own horse, hands tied behind his back, Culhane already tightening the rope around his neck as two of the others held him upright.

"Go!" Culhane shouted, jumping down from a pile of rubble at the mine's opening and slapping Slocum's Appaloosa to get it moving.

And Slocum's horse bolted, tightening that noose around his neck, nearly pulling him off the Appaloosa until the tilted timber suddenly collapsed, freeing the rope and sending Slocum riding off, holding his saddle desperately with his legs while the tightened rope still choked him.

"After him!" Culhane shouted.

Slocum had nearly died. For a moment he thought he had, and he felt himself nearly falling from his horse as unconciousness took him. If that had happened, they would have caught him and finished the job straight away. Only by a gargantuan feat of will did Slocum bring himself back awake, shaking his head violently until the noose thankfully loosened and he was able to breathe again.

Pulling the rope from his neck and throwing it down disdainfully, he straightened on his Appaloosa and tore off into the darkness, the cries of Culhane and his boys already fading behind him.

He'd ridden on, into the night and, he thought, out of Vern Culhane's life . . .

But here he was, involved with the ruthless stranger again. Only this time he vowed to be ready.

Lips pressed tight in determination, Slocum made one more wide, careful sweep around the area before finally heading back to camp.

10

"Mars is up!" the professor shouted excitedly as Slocum rode in and tied up his Appaloosa to the wagon. Grunting, Slocum saw that, indeed, the tiny red dot was just topping the eastern horizon.

The professor immediately swung his telescope that way, adjusting the equatorial mount and switching eyepieces.

"Mr. Slocum," he said with glee.

"That's all right, Professor," Slocum said mildly. "I'll have a look later, if you don't mind. I'd rather just have a smoke right now."

Slocum rolled a quirly and lit it with a lucifer. He thought of firing up one of his few Havanas, but thought he'd save them. The Havanas demanded his attention, and he didn't have it to give to one at the moment. A Havana was an event; a quirly was just a smoke.

"Mr. Slocum, you're fogging my objective lens!" the professor protested.

Slocum saw that, indeed, his smoke was drifting over to the front end of the professor's instrument.

"Sorry," he said, moving to the other side of the camp, where he met Myra, just returning from the darkness.

"Oh!" she said, nearly running into him. For some reason she had a furtive look about her.

"I wouldn't leave the camp if I were you," Slocum said. "It's dangerous out there. Snakes and scorpions, for starters." Slocum regarded her curiously. "What were you doing, if I might ask?"

"Nothing," she said, offering him a quick smile. She seemed preoccupied and tried to move past him.

He took her arm.

"Just be careful, like I said," Slocum repeated.

Her smile was warmer now, and she pressed her hand on his cheek before moving away from him.

"I will, John. Thank you."

Slocum nodded as she moved off.

Curious, he sauntered off the way she had come, but in a moment she had followed him.

"What are you doing?" Myra asked, a bit of apprehension in her voice.

"Just walking."

"Well don't—" she began.

Slocum nearly tripped on something in the near dark; he looked down to see an arrangement of sticks and rocks on the ground, laid out in a pattern of circles.

"What the—"

"Please don't touch it!" Myra said, as Slocum

bent down to pick up a rock. She took it gently from his hand and replaced it.

"Is this what you were doing? Drawing pictures on the desert floor?"

He saw now that the designs were widely scattered, a series of circles and triangles and other odd shapes. Slocum had sometimes seen Indians leave pictures like that in the desert.

"Please, John—it's just . . . something I like to do."

"Well . . ."

Again he bent down, to pick up a stick, but she put her hand on his arms to stop him.

"It's just something I learned in . . . Boston," she said. "Please . . ."

"Well, all right," Slocum said, and allowed her to lead him away.

Suddenly she was smiling up at him, her eyes flashing.

"I can show you something else I learned in Boston," she purred, leading him away from the strange pictures, into the darkness away from camp.

And then her hand was in another place, behind his belt, and pretty soon Slocum had forgotten all about the pictures on the desert floor.

11

Later on, clouds moved in, and, reluctantly, the professor left his telescope behind. Myra had gone off to the wagon to take a nap, and Slocum lit up another quirlie and settled down next to the gentleman on a low rock, after checking for snakes. He chased a baby rattler off into the darkness and settled down, lighting up.

"Perhaps you'd like to try one of these?" the professor said, pulling a fancy-tooled leather cigar case from his pocket and drawing out two rich-looking cigars.

"Havana?" Slocum said, taking one.

"Oh, yes," the professor said. "Best cigars in the world."

"I agree," Slocum said. "You can't beat a Havana."

He pulled out one of his own and handed it to the professor.

"Keep this one for later," Slocum said. "Different brand, but you might like it."

The professor studied the cigar band. "Excellent brand!" he said. "I see you have good taste in tobacco."

"When I can afford it," Slocum said.

Slocum struck a lucifer and gave them both a light.

They smoked in pleased silence for a few moments before the professor opened his sketchbook and attempted to study his latest drawings in the near darkness.

With a sigh, he gave up.

"One doesn't realize how much light the night sky gives out until clouds come," he said. "The moon is the most generous, of course; you could read a book by moonlight. The Milky Way, especially out here, is almost as abundant."

Slocum nodded.

"I do wish the clouds would dissipate," the professor said sadly. "I was obtaining a marvelous sketch of Arabia Terra. That's a vast sandy desert on the Martian surface. My Alvan Clark refractor here is not the best instrument in the world, but this desert environment makes its six-inch aperture seem like ten at least. I'm planning on a much larger instrument, of course, once we find the right sight."

"How big exactly?" Slocum said, enjoying his cigar and the sweet smoke it produced.

"Twenty-four inches at least. That will only be the diameter of the objective lens, of course. The telescope tube itself will be perhaps a hundred feet long."

"A hundred feet!"

"Precisely. It will be housed in a huge dome, of course. Only the finest materials will be used."

Slocum shook his head in wonder. "That's one heck of a project."

"I hope to have the dome completed by the opposition of 1894, four years from now."

"Opposition?"

"When Mars will be closest to Earth. It happens about every two years. But every twenty years or so, Mars is particularly close to our planet, making observations even more critical. You see, I am out to prove that there is life on Mars."

Slocum stopped smoking and looked at the professor in the darkness.

"You mean like vegetables and plants?"

The professor chuckled.

"No, Mr. Slocum. I am convinced that there is *life* on the planet Mars—people like you and me."

Slocum was silent, his original feelings that this man might just be loco beginning to resurface.

"Don't be alarmed, Mr. Slocum. It's perfectly reasonable. After all, Mars is very close to our own planet in composition. Like the Earth, Mars possesses polar ice caps. We are in a desert at this moment, in the Territory of Arizona. On Mars, most of the planet is desert, and this desert is fed by huge canals which bring life-giving water from the polar caps when they melt. At one time Mars may have had abundant water, but over time it has turned into desert. What do you think the government of the United States would do if suddenly the entire country were turned into desert like Arizona? If suddenly the crop lands went parched, the rivers dried up?"

"Well . . . ," Slocum said, thinking. "I suppose they'd try to get water somehow—"

"Precisely! And since the Earth's ocean water is unsuitable for crops and drinking, wouldn't the governments of the world devise a plan for bringing fresh water from the places where it still resided to places where it was needed?"

As Slocum thought about them, the professor's thoughts didn't seem so harebrained.

"I guess they would," Slocum said.

"And since on Mars the fresh water is locked up at the poles in the form of ice, wouldn't it make sense for the Martians to build huge canals to siphon that water down to their crop lands when the polar ice melted in spring?"

Slocum found himself nodding in agreement.

"Well, Mr. Slocum, I have seen those canals! I've drawn them! And therefore, if they exist, and someone built them, doesn't it make sense to conclude that there is intelligent life on the planet Mars?"

"When you put it like that, Professor—"

The other man laughed. "You see? And when I build my observatory out here in the Territory of Arizona, I will be able to see even more proof of the Martians' existence! Perhaps they are even trying to signal us somehow! Perhaps we can help them!"

Suddenly the professor thrust out his hand to Slocum in the darkness.

"Mr. Slocum, I don't think we've been formally introduced. Please stop calling me Professor. It's far too formal, and anyway, though I'm a fellow of the American Academy, to be precise I'm not a professional astronomer but only a wealthy amateur. My name is Percival Lowell, of Boston, Massachussets, and I am going to prove to the world that there is life on the planet Mars!"

12

Ten miles to the south of Slocum's camp, Vern Culhane also regarded the ruddy red dot of Mars in the sky.

So did his three companions. Anyone chancing upon them would have thought that some sort of strange religious rite was under way—and anyone lucky enough to get close to Vern Culhane's visage, to look into his eyes, and live might report that there was almost a look of wistfulness there.

"Slocum's dangerous," Culhane said, finally, turning his eyes from the late night sky to briefly regard the sputtering light of their camp fire. Nearby in scattered plates lay the remains of their bean supper. "We know that already."

"You think it's just chance, him hooking up with those other two?"

"Could be," Culhane said, rubbing a finger lightly over the new scar from Slocum's bullet the night before, not completely covered by his bandanna. "Then again, I don't believe in chance. Anyway, it makes things much harder."

"Why?" another of his companions, a short, balding man sporting a bolo tie, a protuberant belly and a Stetson pushed back on his balding pate, said. "Why don't we just take care of all three of 'em now?"

"It's not that easy," Culhane said. "The girl, of course, we have to be careful with. I think she's the one."

A small gasp came from his companions. The balding one with the belly said, in a hushed voice, "Are you sure?"

"Yes," Culhane said. "She's been leaving signs in the desert. I found one last night, before that little shootout with Slocum. It's her all right."

"How did she get out here?"

"She must have hooked up with that telescope fellow she's with," Culhane said. "We thought by the time she got out here we'd be finished. And now she's hooked up with Slocum . . ."

"This complicates things completely," the last member of their troop, a tall, thoughtful man with eyes as hard as Culhane's, said. It was the first time he had spoken in a while, and the others, even Culhane, gave him their attention.

"You know what we were told," the tall one said evenly. "It has to be a quick operation. Now, suddenly, it's complicated. We knew the girl would try to get help when she got here, but the fact that it's Slocum she turned to can work in our favor. Since we have to eliminate him anyway for coming into contact with us, I suggest we try to isolate him and take care of two problems at once. Without Slocum, the girl

can't stop us. But our mining operations are of
paramount importance, and must be dealt with
immediately."

"When do we get Slocum?"

"I have a plan in mind that will make it simple. I
think 'Vern,' here"—a slight smile of irony crossed
his lips as he pronounced Culhane's name—"and
I can handle Mr. Slocum on our own. The two
of you," he said, indicating the balding fat man
and his companion, "will continue with mining
operations. There's only one mine left on our list,
the Connors Mine, and that has to be the one. You
should be able to check it out in the next couple of
days."

The fat, balding man grumbled, "It's too bad we
didn't keep Slocum around. He did seem to know
what he was doing inside the shafts."

A flash of anger passed across Culhane's face.

"I told you, everyone who sees us here has to
be killed. And Slocum was about to ride off. Are
you second-guessing me?"

The fat man blanched in fear.

"No! I was just . . ." He let the words trail off.

"Never mind that," the tall man said. "Soon-
er or later we would have had to eliminate
Slocum anyway. Seeing how fast he is only
makes me unhappy we botched it the first
time."

He pulled a rolled map from his back pocket and
pressed it flat. He angled it toward the flickering
firelight.

"We will meet—here," he said, indicating a spot, "in two days' time. By then I want everything finished with."

He looked hard at the bald man and his companion.

"Everything," he said.

"I just hope nothing else goes wrong," the fat man said.

They nodded, and watched as the tall man rolled his map back up.

Culhane, who had watched the proceedings with detached interest, said, "Let's hear this plan of yours, 'Ogden.'"

For a moment there was silence, and then the quartet broke out into a staccato of harsh laughter.

"Sure," Ogden said, and with only a fleeting glance at the reddish dot in the sky, the four of them huddled in the night over their schemes.

13

While Culhane schemed, in Flagstaff, a half-breed named Flint, or, as his three Navajo companions called him, Singing Arrow, learned that there was valuable equipment in the desert, and decided to get his hands on it.

Word of the white man from Boston who traveled alone with a woman had been easy enough to get, since Flint was a regular around the saloons of Flagstaff. But he had been even luckier than that, happening to work for the telegraph office as a runner the day after the professor had left with a full wagon.

The telegraph man, a loudmouth named Jorgens, could not be kept quiet about the Easterner who had sent not oné but *fifteen* telegrams in one day—all of them to some college in Boston.

"And all of them are filled with gobbledygook!" Jorgens hooted, holding the stack of message sheets in the air. Since Flint was the only one in the office at the time, lounging in a chair with his boots propped up against the desk, Jorgens turned in his direction and began to read.

" 'Humidity low. Stop. Conditions in area ideal. Stop. Red planet lustrous in sharp black sky. Stop. Boston is soup in comparison.' "

"Soup!" Jorgens guffawed. "The man must be daft! All the rest are the same! Filled with weather and talking about stars! Hell, all you gotta do is look *up* at night to see stars, f'r Pete's sake!"

Flint shrugged.

"Hey, get y'r boots off'n the furniture!" Jorgens shouted, waving the telegram forms at Flint. "How many times I gotta tell you?"

Idly, Flint complied. When Jorgens began to read the telegrams again, Flint, totally bored, got leisurely up from his chair, hitched his pants and headed for the door.

"Hey, where y' going?" Jorgens protested. "I might need you t'run some replies up t' the hotel!"

Flint, running a hand back through his straight, long, black hair, just shrugged and kept walking.

"Stinking half-breed!" Jorgens shouted after him, but he quickly returned to reading the Easterner's telegram forms, for his own amusement.

Flint was nearly out the door when something Jorgens said made him stop.

He turned and walked back into the office.

"Decided to earn a day's pay after all, eh?" Jorgens said.

"What was that last thing you read?" Flint asked.

"What? Oh!" Jorgens held up the form he had been reading from.

" 'Equipment holding up well. Stop. Forward insurance forms for fifty thousand. Be back in Flagstaff by the eighteenth.' "

Jorgens looked up to see Flint once more heading for the door.

"Hey!"

Flint waved idly back and kept walking until he was out the door.

"Stinking half-breed," Jorgens muttered, before he continued to read to himself, hooting in pleasure.

It wasn't long before Singing Arrow had hooked up with his friends camped outside Flagstaff. They'd all been kicked out of the city numerous times, and all were unwelcome in various reservations. One, Golden Eagle, had done hard prison time, and Sheriff Barnes in Flagstaff knew all of them by name and had entertained all but Flint in his jail at one time or another. Only Flint, despite his known connections to the others, had managed to stay out of big trouble. If asked, Sheriff Barnes would have shaken his head in wonder at the boy's fortune.

"Dumb luck," he would have said, though even he thought it was more than that. The boy was quick when he wanted to be, and smart.

Golden Eagle greeted Flint with an upraised palm as he rode his tired old horse into the makeshift campsite—government surplus tents, two with rips that flapped like bird's wings when the wind blew up there, and a few pieces of furniture, mostly stolen.

"Bring any liquor?" Golden Eagle asked, hopefully.

"No."

Golden Eagle's look of disappointment was replaced by one of hope when Flint said, "I've got something better."

"Two bottles?" Kicking Horse said, rising from his tent, one of the ripped ones, and stretching. He wore an odd mix of clothing, part Apache and part U.S. Cavalry, including a vintage blue Civil War cap, which had legitimately been his father's when he scouted for Phil Sheridan during the conflict.

Which hadn't kept his father out of a reservation after the war was won, and hadn't kept him from dying of alcohol poisoning, still bitter at what had been done to him by the government he had helped . . .

Kicking Horse yawned, kept stretching, then advanced.

"I've got a job for us," Singing Arrow said.

"Does it involve liquor?" Golden Eagle laughed.

"All the whiskey you want, when it's over. Fifty thousand dollars in equipment."

His two companions dropped their lazy expressions to regard him with interest. In the other tent another figure stirred but did not rise.

"You're joking," Kicking Horse said finally.

"No," Singing Arrow said, dismounting. He pointed, to nowhere in particular. "Right out there for the taking."

"Where?"

"In the desert. A wagon full of . . . instruments, or something."

"Don't you know?" Golden Eagle said, and now a look of skepticism came over Kicking Horse's face.

"It's there, all right. But it'll only be there for another day or two. It's due back into Flagstaff on the eighteenth."

Kicking Horse yawned again. "So why don't we just wait for it to come back, then steal it when it's in town? Wouldn't be the first time we did a little night work."

Singing Arrow shook his head. "No. We can't be sure of what will happen to it once it gets back to Flagstaff. It might be locked up. Maybe the sheriff'll sleep with it."

Kicking Horse laughed.

Singing Arrow turned his level gaze on the other. "This isn't a joke. I want this done right. Traditional. Like our fathers would have done it."

"What about mothers?" Golden Eagle said, and suddenly Singing Arrow's face reddened.

Kicking Horse stepped in, staring at Golden Eagle. Suddenly he was standing proudly. "Singing Arrow is right." He looked hard at Golden

Eagle. "And it doesn't matter that his mother was white. She was of the tribe. And Singing Arrow is our chief."

For a moment the tension stayed, but then it dissipated, with Golden Eagle suddenly nodding and looking down.

"Let's make preparations," Singing Arrow said. "I want to do this tonight."

The other two moved off, until Golden Eagle stopped and turned.

"Do you want me to wake White Moon?" he said, a touch of a smile accompanying the request, which sounded almost like a taunt.

Singing Arrow began to redden again, but then brought himself under control, locking eyes with Golden Eagle and then smiling broadly.

"No," he said. "*I* will do the waking—as always."

14

In the purpling light of dawn, Slocum sat cleaning his Winchester, and then his Colt. He especially went over the .45 with practiced care, and when he was done, he stood and tested the action of his cross-draw holster.

"Think you're going to need to do that soon?" a sleepy voice said, and Slocum turned to see Myra Hendricks, just having climbed from the wagon and rubbing the sleep from her eyes.

"Why didn't Professor Lowell waken me?" she asked.

Slocum pointed to the now clear sky.

"He said his work was done for the night. Clouds came in and stayed until just before dawn."

She studied the skyline.

"The sky looks like it will stay clear now. Perhaps tonight will be better."

"Tonight is when we'll have trouble," Slocum said.

"Oh?"

Slocum nodded grimly.

"Vern Culhane will be back, I'm sure. And this time he'll have company."

58

"Well, perhaps I could convince the professor to return to Flagstaff."

Slocum nodded. "That would be wise. But it's still a day's ride anyway."

"We should at least get up into the mountains."

"I agree. In fact, I was going to insist. It'll be easier to defend from a high position."

"What makes you so sure Culhane will come?"

Slocum hesitated before answering.

"I can't say, exactly. Let's just say I've met his type before. Bulldog. Won't give up."

Myra nodded thoughtfully. Almost to herself she said, "You seem to know him well."

Slocum's head snapped up in surprise. "You know Vern Culhane?"

As he had seen before, Myra now reacted as if she had been caught in something. "Why, no . . ."

Slocum pressed. "I think you do."

Sighing, Myra said, "Let's just say I've heard of him. From . . . back in Boston."

Still unsure of exactly what to believe, Slocum said, "You know anything about Culhane? What his game is?"

"I only know that he's ruthless." A hard look had come into her fiery eyes, making them almost glow in the morning light. "Very ruthless. You were right, John, when you said he would stop at nothing. He'll never stop until he gets what he wants."

"You seem to know more about him than you're admitting."

Her hard look broke, and she shrugged, turning away.

"Let's just say I've heard of him, and leave it at that."

"I—"

"Please, John," she said, and then she turned away from Slocum, busying herself with making breakfast.

In a short while, over a regenerated fire, Slocum inhaled the strong smell of fresh coffee.

But he continued to check his firearms, even more carefully now, and turned to practice his draw, firing mock volleys into the dawn, the barrel of his deadly Colt pointed dead center at the heart of the rising sun.

15

When Flint entered White Moon's tent, closing the
flap behind him, she was already awake, her blanket pulled up to her chin, staring up at him with
her large brown eyes, which so resembled a deer's,
especially framed as they were in her dark Navajo
face, framed by her long, straight, lustrously silky
black hair. Flint found it easy to believe that she
had been a proud animal in another life, as she
sometimes claimed; indeed, it was her seriousness
that made her so mysterious to him, as well as her
body, which was as sleek as her hair.

"I was listening," she said, her eyes locked onto
his, her mouth set in a grim, straight line.

"You heard?" Flint asked. "And what do you
think?"

"I think what you say has been foretold. Last
night I talked to the wind, and to my sister moon,
and they told me that a breath blows between the
worlds, and that we will see its passing."

As was often the case, Flint had no idea what
she was saying, but the mystery of her words
enthralled him.

"So you think it's a good plan?"

Her eyes didn't waver. "Good or bad, it means nothing. It is meant to be."

A shiver went up Flint's spine.

"You'll come with us?"

"Yes. This was told to me, too. I am to see these things."

"Good," Flint said. For a moment he was at a loss for words.

"And you and I?" he finally said.

Without blinking, without taking her eyes from his, she threw the blanket aside, revealing her nakedness beneath, and said, "This is written also."

Quickly, filled with the terrible need he always felt around White Moon, Flint threw his clothes aside and lay himself on the squaw's cool, long body. Already her nipples were hard, and he tasted first one, then the other. She was a marvelous creature, her belly hard as a stone, the V of her muff soft as a pelt. In a few moments he was already hard and ready, waiting for her to open herself to him.

"White Moon," he moaned.

She took his head between her hands and stared unsmiling into his eyes.

"We are one," she said.

Beneath him, he felt her cool body open, and then suddenly he was inside her hot fire. She was fire and ice, the coolness of her exterior masking the volcano behind her skin. Her muscles tightened around him, and he felt himself sucked deep within her fiery recesses. In a moment he was moving in a jerking rhythm, thrusting deep and then deeper, unable to quiet his cries of abandon as he rose above her, supporting himself on his hands. He had begun to sweat. He looked down into White Moon's face, and saw only the veil of composure she wore always, staring up at him from her huge eyes as only her puffing open mouth moved, suddenly opening wide to let out a gasp of pleasure, before reverting to coolness again.

"White Moon," he panted, his member hard and primed, ready to explode deep within her fire.

"We are—*one*," she gasped.

He came, deep inside her, wave after pumping wave shooting from him to be burned deep within her.

"Yes," she gasped, her huge eyes closing for a moment as the smallest of smiles came onto her straining face.

"Yes."

And then Flint felt her rock beneath him, waves of her orgasm rising over his nearly spent member, pulling the last drop from him into herself.

"Yes . . ."

The waves receded; he began at last to relax within her.

He pulled himself out and lay exhausted next to her on the blanket.

He looked over at her. For a moment she looked straight ahead, at the top of the tent; but then she turned her head, and her huge eyes searched into him, and the slight smile touched her lips again.

"We are one," she whispered, and then looking back at the top of the tent, she added, "and it is written that we will behold the breath that moves between the worlds."

16

By midday, Slocum was frustrated because their progress was slower than he wanted. They were still east of Canyon Diablo by noon, and would not even reach the trail that led up to Flagstaff, at the base of the San Francisco peaks, by nightfall.

Trouble was, the wagon was holding them up. It was not so much the wagon itself, or the mules, but the fact that Professor Lowell's expensive equipment, even though carefully packed, was so delicate that they had to move at a snail's pace to avoid breaking anything.

"That lens cannot be rattled!" the professor shouted at least once every fifteen minutes. "If it's thrown out of alignment, it will take me an entire day just to realign it in the telescope tube! Not to mention the eyepieces!"

The equipment, all of it, was nothing short of a disaster waiting to happen.

"I could never obtain another set of eyepieces like these in the territories! They would have to be sent from Boston, which would take months!"

Slocum had tried taking the reins from the professor, but after a half hour of moaning about eyepieces and alignment and lenses, he had remounted his Appaloosa and given the mules back to Lowell.

By three o'clock, when they had gone barely another two miles past their point at noon, Slocum, in both frustration and in worry that they would not find a suitable spot before dark, said, "I'm riding on ahead."

"My equipment!" the professor cried, which made Myra roll her eyes on the seat next to him.

She looked up at Slocum with a smile and said, "Can I come with you?"

He smiled grimly. "Sorry. But I'll be back."

She nodded.

"See you then."

He turned and kicked his Appaloosa into a gallop, just to leave the wagon, and the complaints issuing from it, behind.

After a mile he slowed, and then stopped long enough to roll a quirly and light it up. He took a draw on the cigarette, tasting the smoke, and blew it out.

Crazy scientist, he thought.

He shook his head, smiling slightly, looking down at his quirly.

But he does like Havanas.

Slocum laughed, and rode slowly on.

By late afternoon, after a bit of worry, he found the spot he wanted. It was perfect, a high rise just miles from the trail leading up to Flagstaff, off to one side and high enough to give him a view to all sides. There were some pines off to the north, which he did not like; but they were far enough away that any trouble that came from that direction could be detected long in advance.

It was even clear enough overhead so that Lowell could set up his equipment—which would keep him quiet, at least.

Satisfied, Slocum marked the path in and then headed back to find the wagon. If they hurried, they could just make it to the new camp by dark. Slocum had deliberately chosen a path without ruts, so that when he took the mule team's reins from the professor again and spurred the mules on, there would be little chance of breaking anything.

Slocum was pleased to find the wagon just where he thought it would be, and doubly pleased to find Lowell just as annoyed by now with their slow progress as Slocum had been when he left them.

"Confound it, we'll never be able to observe tonight!"

"Any trouble?" Slocum asked Myra, riding up alongside the wagon.

She nodded toward the professor. "Only frustration. The weather looks to be perfect tonight, and the professor so wanted to sketch part of the Martian surface that hasn't been visible to us in quite some time."

Slocum touched the brim of his hat.

"I think I can help," he said.

In no time he had convinced Lowell to turn the mule reins over to him and had the wagon on the smooth trail up to the new campsite. Before long, as the sun was setting, they had reached the flat area Slocum had scouted out in the afternoon.

"How's this, Professor?" Slocum said, jumping from the wagon.

Lowell climbed down and surveyed the area. Suddenly he let out a hearty laugh.

"Something wrong?" Slocum asked.

Lowell slapped him on the back.

"Absolutely nothing, Mr. Slocum! Ha!"

"I don't get it."

Lowell led Slocum to the edge of their rise and pointed to the curving valley just below them which stretched out and away before curling up toward the distance again.

"Do you realize where we are, Mr. Slocum?"

"Is it any good for your purposes?"

"More than good! It's one of the landmarks I wanted to visit!"

"Landmark?"

The professor pointed with excitement to the bowl below them.

"It's Meteor Crater, man! The grandest impact basin on the face of the earth!"

"That big scoop in the ground?"

Once again Slocum was beginning to the think the gentleman next to him loco. He'd been by this area once or twice before, but never heard tell about it having anything to do with outer space.

Indicating the sweep of the round depression nearly a mile wide, Lowell said, "Fifty thousand years ago, a mass of iron weighing approximately one million tons slammed into this spot, creating an explosion equal to all the TNT ever detonated on the face of the earth!"

Slocum said nothing, trying to paint a picture of such an explosion in his mind. He found that he couldn't—it was too big.

"That's some bang," he said.

Lowell chuckled. "Yes, some bang indeed! And tomorrow I'd very much like to explore the floor of that crater!"

"Whatever you like," Slocum said.

Lowell was already at the back of the wagon, excitedly unpacking his telescope tube from its flannel wrappings.

"And now," Lowell said, "we have just enough light to get set up! And then—a marvelous night of seeing!"

Slocum looked up to see Myra suddenly at his side.

"Perhaps, John," she said, smiling up at him, "a marvelous night for other things as well?"

17

Myra was right; it did prove a good night for other things besides looking through telescopes. The woman was nearly insatiable, and knew tricks even Slocum hadn't thought of. It was just at the point where Slocum was ready to yell uncle that the professor called her and she had to hurry off.

"But there's always tomorrow night," she said, smiling, her eyes still fiery as she stroked Slocum's cheek before going to see what the professor needed.

Slocum found himself marveling at her once more. She was almost too perfect, her body devoid of flaws to the point where that almost seemed a flaw in itself. And there was still something about those fire-filled eyes that burned too bright and seemed to know much more than they were telling . . .

Slocum dressed, smoked a quirly a respectful distance from the professor's equipment and then approached the telescope.

Lowell was alone.

"Myra go to take a nap?"

"Yes," the professor said. "It's one of the only times I've ever seen her even a little tired. Usually I have to force her to sleep."

Slocum smiled to himself.

So she'd been worn out, after all.

"Anything interesting in the sky?" Slocum asked.

"Certainly! The Xanthe Terra region of Mars is visible tonight—and I'm certain I see patches of vegetation lining its borders!" He sighed in frustration. "If only I had access now to a larger instrument! In this climate I could almost see their cities!"

"So you're sure there are creatures on the planet Mars?"

"More than certain, Mr. Slocum! As I told you, they have built a giant irrigation system to replenish their lowlands with water. The fruits of their labor are obvious. Patches of green vegetation become visible each Martian spring, grown from the water the Martians have siphoned from the polar caps!"

Lowell stood aside for Slocum to look.

Once again he saw a fuzzy reddish disk with a white cap tilted toward him, a few darkish spots, nothing more.

"Can you see the canals now, Mr. Slocum?"

"Still can't seem to make them out, Professor."

Lowell sighed. "I admit it takes training of the eye to see these things. Try this. Instead of looking straight into the eyepiece, avert your vision. Move your eye so that you are looking into the ocular from the side. This is a common astronomer's trick, since the most sensitive part of the eye is not in the center. You can see better in the dark with this so-called 'averted vision.'"

Shrugging, Slocum tried what the professor said. Indeed, he could see a little more, but it was just more of the same fuzziness with light and darker patches.

He stood away from the telescope, shaking his head.

"Mind if I ask you something, Professor?"

"Not at all!"

"Now, don't get cussing at me—but is it possible you're seeing what you want to?"

For the first time since he had met the man, Slocum sensed anger rising in the professor's visage. With effort, the other man kept it down, though.

"I see what I see, Mr. Slocum."

"Suit yourself. I meant nothing by it."

"I realize that. But you must understand that I have faced this sort of attitude since the beginning of my Martian studies. I should be used to it, but I'm not. I want everyone to see as I do, and to realize that there certainly *is* life on the planet Mars."

"I never said there wasn't," Slocum said. "It's just that I'm having trouble seeing it with my own eyes."

"Well," the professor said, his spirits restored, slapping Slocum lightly on the back, "when my

observatory is built in the Territory, you shall
have a special invitation to come and look through
the twenty-four-inch lens, and *then* perhaps you
will see!"

"Fair enough, Professor."

Lowell rubbed his eyes and stepped away from
the instrument.

"Time for a good cigar, Mr. Slocum? I sniffed
your rather inferior cigarette a little while ago."

Slocum's face split into a grin.

"Always time for a Havana," he said.

18

After they had lit up, Slocum striking a lucifer for both of them, Slocum said, "Mind if I ask you another question, Professor?"

"Not at all, Mr. Slocum—that's what cigars are for!"

Slocum smiled. "I was just curious about Myra."

"Miss Hendricks?" the professor said in surprise. "What about her?"

"Where did you find her?"

"In Boston, of course!"

"Did you seek her out?"

The professor rubbed his chin.

"No . . . Actually, she found me. I was looking for an assistant, and she appeared in my office one day. I hadn't even advertised, come to think of it. She just . . . appeared in the right place at the right time, so to speak."

"Did you . . ." Slocum didn't quite know how to say it. "Did you check her out at all?"

"Whatever do you mean?"

"References, anything like that?"

74

Again the professor rubbed his chin, seemed to be surprised.

"Actually . . . no. Although normally that would have been essential. As I remember, she was so thoroughly knowledgeable and proficient that I hired her on the spot!"

Slocum smiled to himself, thinking that to some men, one look at Myra's shape would have been enough incentive to hire her, but he said nothing, because he knew that to the professor such a thought would only be puzzling. When the professor said Myra knew her stuff, he meant she knew telescopes and charts and all the rest that so enthralled Lowell.

"Is there something bothering you, Mr. Slocum?" Lowell asked.

"Not really. It's just that—did you ever think that maybe she's *too* good to be true?"

"Whatever do you mean? In science, you either know what you are about or you don't—there's little room for subjectivity."

"Never mind, then."

"You know," Lowell said, pondering, "I believe I do know what you mean. In a way, she *is* awfully knowledgeable about my work. To be truthful, I was rather pleased that she had studied it so closely. She seemed to be even one step ahead of me on some points, as a matter of fact. She's a very bright girl."

"Yes."

"But believe me, I merely consider myself fortunate. She's an extremely able assistant—"

Overhead, somewhat north of Mars, a distant light flashed, then was suddenly gone.

"What was that?" Slocum said.

The professor was staring at the spot.

"Truthfully, I don't know. We've been seeing strange lights like that ever since we came out here. It's been a few nights since they've appeared, but despite hard thought, I can't explain them. Some sort of illusion, perhaps, or an unknown astronomical phenomenon. Believe me, Mr. Slocum, there's plenty in the sky that science has not been able to fully explain—"

Again a light flashed, to the east of the first one, and then there was a streak of light that stopped, flashed and disappeared.

"Fascinating," Lowell said. "Something like a meteor—"

Slocum stood up.

"You mean like that one that smashed into that crater below?" he said.

Lowell chuckled, taking Slocum by the arm and making him sit down again.

"Don't be alarmed, Mr. Slocum. The chances of another fragment from outer space hitting this spot are . . . astronomical. It won't happen, I can assure you. We are perfectly safe here . . . as far as meteors are concerned." Lowell frowned. "However, I'm not at all sure that what we just witnessed was a meteor—"

Something very familiar—and earthly—rang out: a gunshot.

"Down!" Slocum said, forcing Lowell to the dirt.

"Mr. Slocum, my instruments—"

"Where the sky is concerned, you know what you're doing, Professor—but where bullets come in, *I'm* the expert."

Slocum made sure the professor stayed flat on the ground.

"Myra!" Slocum called out.

In the wagon there was a stirring, just as another shot split the darkness. Slocum placed the general direction.

"Myra, stay where you are!"

"I will!" the answer came.

"I've had enough of this," Slocum vowed, crawling away from Lowell to the wagon, where his Appaloosa was tied. Standing in a crouch, he unslung his Winchester from its scabbard and then moved quickly to the lip of their rise. From below, in the bowl of the meteor crater, silence reigned until yet another gunshot sounded.

"Slocum!" a voice, Vern Culhane's, called. "Slocum, come on down and get me!"

Another rifle shot, and now Slocum aimed his Winchester at the spot.

"Slocum—!"

Slocum fired, and a cry came from below.

"Did you get him, Mr. Slocum?" Lowell whispered from behind him.

Slocum listened to the silence from below.

"I don't know," he said grimly, "but I'm going down to find out."

19

With great caution born of experience, Slocum began the long climb down into the crater. It was hazardous in the dim light, but there were plenty of handholds, and Slocum had done much mountain scaling that was worse.

All the while he listened. Still there was no sound—not a horse, not the wheeze of a wounded man.

Slocum could not quite believe that he had managed a deadly hit with the first shot. From his years of experience in sharpshooting, he knew that luck had very little part in the business of hitting a target. Skill—and caution—were much more important than luck—and more constant friends.

Still, Slocum heard nothing.

Halfway down the crater, nearing the spot where he had pinpointed Culhane, a sudden thought assaulted Slocum. What if he had been lured down here deliberately? What if—

Quickly, with little regard for his own safety now, Slocum reached the spot where he had fired at Culhane.

There was no one there—no horse, no wounded or dead opponent.

There was, however, a sign that Culhane had been there—a fresh bandanna, unmarked by blood, left, deliberately no doubt, under a rock.

"Find my gift, Slocum?" a mocking voice came from above.

Immediately Slocum turned and aimed to fire—but he saw in the shadowed night illumination Vern Culhane, standing at the top of the crater, holding Myra Hendricks before him as a shield.

"Go ahead, Slocum—shoot me!"

Culhane laughed.

Slocum lowered his rifle.

It was then that he did hear a slight sound—one that saved his life.

He dropped to the rocky floor of the crater just as a gunshot sounded very close by.

Unthinking, becoming the animal that holds a gun and is interested only in self-preservation, Slocum, in one smooth motion, dropped his Winchester and drew his Colt across his body, firing even as the draw was made.

A wide, flashing arc of five bullets split the night, and in its illumination Slocum saw the man he had hit, in the process of firing at him again, and, from some far-off place, he heard the man's cry as he was hit twice in the chest.

The man's hands flew back, wanting to stem the flow of blood even as he was dead, drilled through the heart. Then Slocum was already advancing on

his opponent, the sixth bullet in his Colt ready to
fire if needed, which it was not.

Slocum stood over the body, which twitched once
and then was still.

It looked like one of Culhane's companions.

From up above, Slocum heard a cry of
anguish.

"Now, Slocum, you will pay with more than
your life!"

Culhane stood there, still shielded by Myra.

"I swear to the heavens to make you pay,
Slocum!" Culhane screeched, in an almost inhu-
man voice.

Then he pulled Myra away from the crater's
lip.

Quickly, leaving the dead body behind, Slocum
retrieved his Winchester and reloaded his Colt
as he climbed. He slipped once, trying to do too
much at once, and stopped to finish his reloading,
pushing the 44–40 caliber bullets into place. He
held the Colt ready in his right hand and forced
himself up the steep slope.

When he reached the top, rolling up over the lip
of the crater, he threw his Winchester to the right
as a diversion and came up ready with his Colt.

But, as he had feared, the camp was
silent.

By the tripod of the telescope lay a figure, and
for a moment a lump climbed into Slocum's throat.
He feared he had failed in his mission. If Lowell
were dead—

Then Slocum heard a moan, and the professor rolled over and sat up, bumping momentarily into his tripod, throwing it nearly off balance.

Lowell held his head.

"Mr. Slocum—?" he asked groggily.

"Yes," Slocum said.

"A . . . man came. I tried to defend Myra, but—"

"You did just fine, Professor," Slocum said, helping him to his feet.

Lowell looked around.

"Oh, dear—she's been kidnapped!"

"Yes, Professor, I'm afraid she has been."

Slocum retrieved his Winchester and pressed it into the scientist's hands.

"You'll have to be ready with this—though I don't think any of them will come back."

"Mr. Slocum," Lowell said, still groggy.

Slocum squeezed the man's arm.

"Just stay here, and stay ready, and I'll be back as soon as I can. Before noon tomorrow, at the latest."

"You'll rescue her, Mr. Slocum?"

Slocum's face was set.

"I'll do everything I can, Professor."

20

In the night, there were distant shots, and White Moon stopped the others.

"Wait," she said, holding her hand up. "And listen."

Their band of four stopped. They had left the ponderosa pines of Flagstaff behind hours ago, taking the long, gentle slope down, from the forrested plateau where the city nestled, into the sage plains of the desert. Only the stars had been their companions, and the moon, and they stood now in native dress, except for Kicking Horse, who still wore his motley uniform of U.S. Cavalry and Indian clothing.

"There," Flint—or Singing Arrow, as they now proudly called their leader—said, pointing to the east as another shot rang out. "That is the direction."

"The bowl," Golden Eagle said. "Listen to the echo."

White Moon, her eyes closed, holding her hands out to the sky, said, "Yes."

Suddenly she opened her doe's dark eyes and began to walk onward.

"We'll never reach it by daylight," Golden Eagle grumbled.

"No matter," White Moon said. "What we seek will be waiting there for us."

After hesitating for a moment, and waiting for Singing Arrow's nod, the three men followed White Moon.

Deep in the night, hours after the gunshots, after passing through Walnut Canyon, they stopped again.

Singing Arrow almost said they should proceed, but White Moon held up her hand, looking to the sky, and said, "Watch."

They were quiet, and regarded the sky, and then they saw.

There were lights. Up deep in the clouds of the Milky Way at first, a spot of illumination and then another flew downward and brightened. Then there were others, ringing the moon, and then many around the planet Mars, seeming to dance to an unknown drumbeat.

Singing Arrow could almost hear it—and he knew White Moon could, because her body swayed, her hands held up to the moving stars, and now she began to chant, in a tongue that was not native and which Singing Arrow did not know.

"White Moon," he said.

"Be quiet," she whispered to him, and then continued the chant, as the lights played in the air.

Fascinated at first, but growing impatient, Golden Eagle finally said, "This is foolish. We should go on."

White Moon ignored him, her eyes closed, waving her hands gently as if swayed by a breeze.

"She is loco," Golden Eagle said. He pointed at Singing Arrow. "And so are you for listening to her!"

Singing Arrow glowered at him.

Golden Eagle grabbed at his crotch and looked steadily into Singing Arrow's face. "Or is it down here that she holds you, *Chief*?"

Suddenly Singing Arrow and Golden Eagle were both on their feet, facing each other.

"I think it is because she would not share her bed with *you*," Singing Arrow spat.

Through it all, White Moon, eyes closed, chanted and swayed.

Kicking Horse stepped between the two men.

"Stop it—"

Golden Eagle threw him aside.

"Stay out of it. This is between the *half-breed* and me."

Kicking Horse, rising, said, "Don't do this! We are all brothers!"

"I don't think so," Golden Eagle spat, his eyes locked on Singing Arrow.

Suddenly two knives were drawn, their blades glowing in the light of the stars.

"Stop," White Moon said, and the tone of her voice made the two angry warriors look her way.

Her soft, large eyes looked at them, her mouth grim and set.

"Look," she said, pointing upward.

They looked up into the night sky, and gasped.

The two knives fell to the ground.

Above them the stars, the night, danced, lights alive and moving—and then suddenly a light dropped down toward them, hovering, flashing . . .

"The breath that moves between worlds," White Moon whispered.

Thoughts of fighting, for the moment, were forgotten, and they watched in fascination, before the light pulled away back into the night, and they walked on.

21

Tied across the back of Vern Culhane's horse, Myra Hendricks feigned unconsciousness.

Which was a wise move, because for a few miles Culhane was all but filled with madness. Myra thought he was capable of anything—indeed, she already knew that he was capable of anything.

But for those miles Culhane was content merely to ride as fast as the night and his horse would allow, and to curse the heavens and John Slocum.

"He'll die slow," Culhane spat, "as slow as I can make him. There are plenty of ways. One of my men! *My men!* He has to pay, and he'll pay long and slow."

Myra could feel the man's anger, trussed and laid across his saddle behind him as she was. Culhane was tight as a spring, and liable to burst at any time.

But all he did was ride. And after a time Myra came to realize that Culhane was afraid of John Slocum.

A secret smile crossed her features.

So, she thought, I was right about John Slocum from the beginning.

And this knowledge made the ride easier.

Sometime after sunup Culhane finally stopped at a creek, letting the horse rest and drink. He climbed down from the saddle and went to the water himself, throwing some into his face.

Stealing a look at him, Myra could see that Culhane's anger had not slackened.

Suddenly he stood straight and came back to her.

"Wake up," he said roughly, and as Myra closed her eyes, she felt the slap of his hand across her face.

In a moment he was untying her from the saddle and dragging her off, laying her in a heap on the ground.

He kicked dirt at her.

"Wake up!" he repeated.

Her eyes slitted to see what he would do next. She faked coming out of unconsciousness when she saw his boot pulled back to kick her.

"Ohhhhhh . . ."

"Wake up!" Culhane said, pulling her into a sitting position and forcing her back against a rock.

Myra opened her eyes and regarded him.

"So," Culhane said, a sinister smile doing nothing to relieve the cruelty of his features.

"Yes, we meet," Myra said. *"Vern Culhane,"* she added, sarcastically.

"And what do you call yourself here?" Culhane asked.

"My name is Myra Hendricks."

Culhane laughed harshly.

"A good Boston name, no doubt."

She nodded. "It was found in a birth register there, and there's a history to Myra Hendricks, in case anyone is curious."

Culhane spat.

"They're not smart enough to be curious here."

Myra gave him a tiny smile.

"John Slocum is smart enough."

For a moment she thought she had made a mistake; the coiled spring was about to lash out, his face filling with rage and remembrance. As he drew his hand back to strike her, his fingers played over the new scar on his forehead, creased by the bullet Slocum had sent his way in the dark two nights before.

"You wouldn't dare strike me," Myra said.

For the briefest time his anger even increased, but he held his hand and his anger.

"Not now," he said. "There'll be time for more than that later."

She laughed.

"You're a fool here, just as you were a fool at home."

"You think me a fool now, but after our operations are completed—"

"No one gave you *authority* to do what you're doing! You were turned down!"

"They were wrong."

"How dare you say that!" Now color rose to her own perfect cheeks, and anger stirred up from her own breast. "You had no right!"

"So they sent you after me," Culhane said, snorting. "A woman—"

"More than that, and you know it."

Culhane made a mock bow.

"Of course—Your *Highness*."

"When we return home, you will be punished."

"If I return home in triumph, you will be ousted, and I will be a hero."

"Heroes don't go to prison—but criminals do."

He stared at her hard, before looking at the ground.

Briefly, then, she had gotten through to him.

"And John Slocum," she said, tauntingly.

"Slocum will die!" Culhane spat. "I will kill him with my own hands!"

His growing anger haulted, and he looked into her fierce eyes with new knowledge.

"So . . ."

"What is it?" she asked.

"I understand your feelings for Slocum now."

She put a look of pride on her face, but her cheeks were reddened just the same.

Suddenly he was looming over her, his anger turned to something else. His sinister smile was back. He leaned down very close to her.

She lowered her eyes, but he lifted her chin and looked into her eyes.

She spat at him.

He wiped at the spot, laughing.

"Perhaps you can be redeemed."

"Where are the rest of your men?" she asked quickly, trying to distract him.

He smiled.

"They're close enough. At the Connors Mine, finding what we came here for."

Suddenly he was horribly close, leaning down over her, pushing her back.

"Even if you could, you wouldn't dare," she said, with fear for the first time creeping into her voice.

"Oh?" Culhane said. "There's something about this climate—"

Desperate, she had a sudden thought.

"Then untie me," she purred, letting a smile soften her lips. "There *is* something about this climate—"

Producing a long blade, very close, his craggy, hard face even with hers, Culhane suddenly reached around to cut through her bonds, freeing her hands.

"And my feet?" Myra purred, pressing herself up at him as one hand searched desperately the ground beneath her, searching for what she hoped was there and then finding it.

"Yes, Your Highness," Culhane said, reaching down to slice through the ropes binding her.

"Ahh . . ." Myra said, letting Culhane drop the blade as he lowered himself down to her.

"And now . . ." Culhane said.

"Yes, now!" Myra said, pushing the rock she had found up into his face, pulling her hand back and then hitting him again.

With a choking cry, Culhane fell to the side as Myra hit him yet a third time, dazing him.

In a flash Myra was up and racing for Culhane's horse, which was still drinking at the creek. Quickly Culhane gathered his wits and was up, chasing her.

Pulling herself up into the saddle, Myra shouted to the horse, "Go!" and kicked her heels into its sides.

Its mouth still dripping water, the startled beast set off.

Culhane, running madly, watched in raging anger as the laughing young woman dashed off, leaving him behind.

He stopped, his anger giving rise to a horrible screeching cry, "Now you, like Slocum, will die slow!"

22

Slocum was about as angry as he ever had been with himself.

What was wrong with him? Usually he was smart enough to know what had to be done and then do it. He prided himself on his caution.

After all, hadn't caution been all that had saved his skin all these years? If not for caution, he would have rotted away in some federal prison years ago, or been buried on some boot hill or in some shallow grave or left on the rocks to be picked at by turkey buzzards.

What was wrong with him?

Was he getting soft, or old?

No, it was something else.

Ever since he'd hooked up with the professor and Myra, he felt as if he weren't quite in control of things. And now this unnerved him. He hadn't noticed it before, but the last couple of days had been two of the strangest he'd ever lived. It was as if someone had been pulling the strings for him.

It was a scary thought, but he knew now it was true. Ever since he had hooked up with Myra—

The woman was it. There was something mighty strange about her. Sure, she was good to look at, and mighty good to love, but Slocum now felt, on reflection, that he had seen only the top layer of the onion, and that there were plenty of other skins below the one she showed him.

And it wasn't just that she was a lady. Plenty of ladies had come Slocum's way, and a lot of them had turned his head—but this was different.

It was something about the night, Slocum decided. The nighttime was too unpredictable.

Too many strange things happened in the night.

It was too capricious, as he had thought before. A man could be riding along under cloak of darkness, thinking himself safe, and the coyotes and rattlesnakes would be eyeing him right and left, just waiting for their chance.

A man couldn't tell where he was, and what was happening.

No, Slocum decided, he didn't think he liked the night after all.

In fact, he'd had enough of it.

A tough, hard look came onto Slocum's face.

The problem, he figured, was a simple one, as most problems were.

He had to find Myra, and fight it out with Culhane and his men.

Then he would get the professor and Myra to Flagstaff, and be done with them.

Be on his way.

And do the rest of his riding by day, if he could help it.

He'd never ride at night again.

His mind made up, he rolled a quirly, lit it using one hand and found for his horse a long, even slope down into the crater.

Slocum was startled to find that the body of the man he'd shot was gone.

He knew he had the place; he'd marked it in his mind and with Culhane's bandanna, but though the bandanna was still there, the body had disappeared.

In the growing light of dawn, Slocum dismounted and searched the area. No sign of another rider. But maybe someone had come in on foot and carried the body off.

Slocum widened his search, figuring that even someone on foot would have left a sign, or possibly would have tied a horse some distance from the site.

A good half mile away, up the slope of the crater, he found a tied horse, badly saddled. This had obviously been the rider's mount.

Slocum fixed the saddle, tied the horse behind his own and continued to search.

There was nothing else. Nothing.

Then Slocum had a sudden thought.

No more mistakes, he said to himself, looking up at the top of the crater, near where he had left the professor.

No more nighttime muddleheadedness.

In resolve, Slocum threw his quirlie down, remounted and climbed slowly back up the hill of the crater.

23

"Mr. Slocum!"

The professor looked up in surprise as Slocum rode slowly back into camp, trailing a new horse behind his own.

"Why, I thought you said you'd be back much later—have you found something already?"

Slocum hid a smile at the sight of Lowell standing like a sentry in front of his telescope, rifle at the ready. Slocum knew his decision to return now had been a good one. If any trouble had come, Lowell would have been overpowered in ten seconds flat.

"No, Professor, I haven't found anything yet. I've just cleared my head out and decided it best we stay together. Let's just call it a hunch that it would be a good idea."

Slocum saw an almost imperceptible sigh of relief issue from the scientist.

"Well, I can't say I'm sorry to see you back. Every sound I've heard since you left has startled me. And I certainly haven't been able to concentrate on my work—"

Slocum noted the open notebook on its table.

"Time to clear out of here, Professor," Slocum said. "What I'd like to do is pack all your equipment up safely and hide it nearby." Slocum nodded at the horse tied behind his. "We can move much more quickly on horseback."

Still clutching the rifle, Lowell began to nod.

"Yes, yes, I suppose you're right. But my instruments . . ."

"Can't be helped. I think you'd agree that the most important thing now is to get Myra back."

"Of course," the professor said quickly. But there was still a wistful look on his face.

"We'll get back to your instruments as soon as we can."

Lowell's face stiffened.

"You're completely right, Mr. Slocum. And we should get moving as soon as possible."

Slocum got down from his Appaloosa and gently took the rifle from the scientist's hands.

"Let me worry about the Winchester, Professor," he said, kindly.

Lowell nodded. "Yes, of course," he said and hurried off to gather the felt coverings for his instruments.

In an hour, as the sun had well topped the eastern horizon, they were ready to go.

They had packed the wagon, covered it with a tarp and coaxed the mules into pulling it off to the side of the road, under the faint camouflage of some low brush.

As they mounted their horses, the professor looked down at the badly hidden, still visible wagon and sighed.

"It's the best we could do, I suppose . . ."

"Yes," Slocum said. "And now it's time to ride."

"Yes," Lowell said sadly, and they pulled their mounts around and rode off, the professor looking back once, sighing, before they had left the wagon behind.

Slocum said, "We're going to track Vern Culhane. He may have got out fast, but I think we can find him."

"And Myra, of course?"

Slocum nodded. "That's the plan, Professor. From what I know of Culhane, he would have killed her here if he was going to kill her at all. So I'm betting she's still alive and well. Culhane wants me, we know that, so we're going to give him a chance to get me—"

"You're not going to put yourself in danger, are you, Mr. Slocum?"

Slocum smiled grimly.

"Not if I can help it. But if he knows we're following him, he might slow down to face me. Then we can get Myra back."

Lowell shook his head.

"I don't know, Mr. Slocum . . ."

"Look, Professor," Slocum said, "to be honest, if I had the time, or the way, I'd get you off in some safe place and do this on my own. But too much can go wrong out here. So we stay together." He hardened his voice just a bit. "And we do it my way."

"Of course! Of course!" the professor said. "It's just that I don't like the idea of you putting yourself in danger on our account."

"Do you have a better idea on how to save Myra?" Slocum asked.

The professor frowned, and then shook his head.

"I see what you mean, Mr. Slocum. Let's proceed."

"That's just what we're going to do."

In less than an hour Slocum had picked up the trail of Vern Culhane's horse. There was only one set of tracks, which meant that Culhane had ridden with Myra behind him.

In another two hours they had found Culhane's camp.

The signs of struggle were obvious.

Slocum studied the area closely, then concluded with a smile, "She got away."

"Splendid!" Lowell said.

Slocum went on, "There's a set of horse tracks leading a little north of the way we came, but my guess is Myra made a circle and headed back for the wagon at Meteor Crater. Someone else— Culhane—headed out by foot to the east."

"What do we do, Mr. Slocum?"

Slocum answered immediately, "As much as I'd like to go after Culhane, I think we'd better head back and hook up with Myra. Then we're taking you and Myra and your wagon up to Flagstaff as fast as possible so I can come back out here and clear this business with Culhane up once and for all."

Lowell had already turned his horse back the way they had come.

"I'm not going to protest your plan, Mr. Slocum," Lowell said. "I've had enough adventure in the desert, and I've taken more than enough measurements to know that my observatory should be built somewhere near Flagstaff itself. The elevation—"

The professor was startled when Slocum suddenly pulled his Winchester and said, "Get down."

"But—"

"We've got company," Slocum said.

As the professor dismounted, the first shot rang out, from across the creek. Then another.

"Two rifles," Slocum said, pulling Lowell to the safety of some low rocks by the bank of the nearby creek. Beyond the water two more gunshots erupted.

"They're dumber than I thought," Slocum said. "Didn't cover the area to the east. Unless—"

Slocum frantically scanned the brush and low rocks behind them and saw the muzzle of a rifle pointed their way. He threw himself on Lowell and

fired off a shot from the Winchester as a rifle shot
rang out overhead.

"They're not quite as stupid as I'd hoped,"
Slocum said.

24

Vern Culhane's anger had not had time to dissipate as he walked off into the desert, but then a sight met his eyes that nearly made him smile. There, riding toward him like a mirage, were his other two companions. In no time at all they were reunited.

The fat, balding man sporting a bolo tie and Stetson pushed back on his head looked down at Culhane, puzzled. The other, a bland-faced man, seemed nevertheless excited.

Before the fat one could speak, Culhane said, " 'Ogden' is dead."

"Was it Slocum?" the fat one asked.

"Yes, Slocum did it. I had the woman, but . . ."

The two looked at him expectantly.

"It's no matter," Culhane said. He turned to regard the bland fellow, who seemed about to explode with news. "Well?"

"We found what we need, just like we thought."

"Lots of it," the fat man interjected.

The bland one rushed on, excited. "More than we'll ever require!"

Still fumbling, the bland one reached into a saddlebag, pulled a lump of pitchblende out and threw it down to Culhane.

"You can see the ore in there," the bland man said.

Culhane examined the pitchblende closely and spotted the mineral he was looking for in it.

He nodded, handing the sample back up.

"You say there's plenty?"

"Yes, and it'll be easy to get out and process."

"Good work." He briefly touched the scar on his head, the healing furrow in it.

"Now I've got another job for us."

The bland one and the fat man looked down at him expectantly.

Culhane said, "It's a simple one. We wait."

The two men climbed down from their horses and did as they were told.

"Just like I wanted," Culhane said an hour later. As he had thought, Slocum had tracked him to his campsite. Now he could finish Slocum off and be done with him.

For good.

From across the river, behind Slocum and the scientist, Culhane made a motion to the two others.

In a moment the shooting began.

25

There was just enough cover behind the V of rocks Slocum had shoved the professor into to cover them, and for Slocum to go to work.

"Just stay down, and stay quiet, Professor," Slocum said.

Lowell, as flat on the ground as a man could get, looked up at Slocum in alarm.

"You won't get an argument from me, Mr. Slocum."

"Good."

A slight smile came to Slocum's lips. There was something about action that made a man see more clearly. For the first time since he had hooked up with Myra and the professor, Slocum felt fully alert.

There were two opponents about thirty yards away, across the creek, and a single shooter behind them. Slocum guessed the single shooter would be Culhane.

As if reading Slocum's thoughts, Vern Culhane shouted out, "Slocum! You about ready to die?"

Slocum said nothing, but paid attention to his Winchester.

Culhane cracked a shot off the rock overhead, and Slocum waited until the other two
had fired.

A two-second delay, then three seconds for the
two of them to get off their shots.

Then Slocum lifted his Winchester without rising and fired a shot into the air.

Instantly there was reaction.

Again Culhane shot, and then the other two
fired shots off.

Again, two seconds and about three seconds.

Slocum had what he needed now.

He edged himself around until he was facing
the two shooters across the water. A final time
he checked his Winchester.

All was ready.

Slocum fired a single shot into the air.

From behind him Culhane shot, chipping a piece
of rock.

Slocum counted to two, and as the other two
shooters were pulling off their shots Slocum
pushed himself up out of the V and fired.

As he had expected, the two men out in the
desert were big targets.

Slocum pulled off two rifle shots, then two
more.

Instantly one of the men, a fat man wearing
a bolo tie, threw his rifle aside. Slocum saw his
first shot knock the man's Stetson from his head.
The second shot blossomed in red on the man's
chest.

The second shooter in the desert was hit in the shoulder. Slocum heard him grunt and drop to the ground, even as the fat man was falling, dead.

Slocum was back behind the confines of the V, even as Culhane reacted by firing.

"You're going to die, Slocum!"

"I doubt it, Culhane!" Slocum answered. "Better ask your men about dying!"

"Vern!" came a weak cry from out in the desert. It was the man Slocum had winged.

"Vern, he got me good! I need help!"

"Keep firing!" Culhane ordered angrily.

Culhane fired at Slocum and the professor again, shattering rock.

"Vern, I'm coming out!" the wounded man said.

"I said stay where you are!"

"I can't! Vern—!"

Slocum heard a shot, and ventured a look around the edge of the V. He saw the second man in the desert clutch his chest where he stood, going down as Culhane shot him.

The man staggered forward, before a rifle shot chipped rock near Slocum's head, and he drew it back into the shelter of the V.

"You're still gonna die, Slocum!" Culhane shouted.

Slocum reacted to the sound of the scuffle of rocks just in front of him, and looked up to see the man Culhane had just shot stumble toward him, one hand over his bleeding chest, the other held out in supplication.

"Slocum—" the man gasped.

The man suddenly stumbled forward, falling into the rock shelter, dead on top of Slocum.

Slocum heard Culhane laugh, heard him move.

Desperately Slocum pushed at the dead body.

The professor helped, and in a few seconds they had pushed the dead man aside.

Slocum jumped to his feet, Winchester ready and turning to aim at the figure of Vern Culhane, laughing, on the back of one of two horses, obviously those of his companions, which had been hidden in nearby brush.

Culhane rode low, continuing to laugh as he used the brush as cover.

Slocum fired off one shot, two, but both missed.

Culhane's horse carried its laughing rider away.

"You're still gonna die, Slocum!"

And then the laughter, and Culhane, were gone.

26

Instantly Slocum knew he had two choices.

Either he could go for Culhane now and leave the professor behind, or get the professor back to Myra, and the two of them to Flagstaff, and then track Culhane down at his leisure.

Nearly every fiber of his being told him to go after Culhane now. He knew it might take a while; he guessed Culhane's horse would be better rested than his own Appaloosa, and Culhane would use every trick at his disposal to try to lose Slocum. Culhane was no fool; he had proved that. He had already caught Slocum twice, and it would be no Sunday picnic hunting him down.

But . . .

With a sinking feeling, knowing what he had to do, Slocum turned to tell Professor Lowell that it was time to get him back to his beloved equipment, back to his assistant and back to Flagstaff and safety.

With a start of surprise, Slocum saw that Lowell was already mounted, and had the reins of Slocum's Appaloosa in his hand.

The scientist, with a passionate look in his eyes, handed the reins down to Slocum and said, "Mr. Slocum—what are we waiting for!"

"What—?"

"Let's ride that man down!"

"But, Professor—"

Without another word, Lowell left the reins in Slocum's hand and kicked his own mount into a full gallop, heading in the direction Vern Culhane had gone.

"Well damn . . . ," Slocum said, another smile finding its way onto his still-surprised face.

This Professor Lowell was just full of surprises.

Spurring his own horse, Slocum had caught up with Professor Lowell a few moments later.

"Where did you learn to ride like that?" Slocum called over, noting the professor's expertise in staying with a horse at full gallop.

"Boston, in my youth!" Lowell shouted. He was hunched forward in the saddle, teeth to the wind, smiling broadly under his mustache. "We all had to ride—my sister Amy, too! I always wanted to ride like this, but our teacher, Miss Halber, never would let us! But Amy and I would often sneak out and let the horses have their run of it!"

The professor laughed, throwing his head back, and whooped.

"Professor, we'll make a cowboy of you yet!" Slocum said.

Lowell whooped again, and spurred his horse onward.

But after two hours they had found nothing.

Slocum stopped them three times, sure that he had found Culhane's trail. But each time he came up cold.

"I just don't get it," Slocum said. "It's like he rode off into thin air."

After the third of these defeats, Slocum climbed back into his saddle and said, "Well, that's it. We've got darkness coming in a couple of hours, and I want you back to your instruments by then."

Lowell said, "Please don't worry about my observations, Mr. Slocum."

"It's not that," Slocum said. "It's Miss Hendricks I'm worried about."

Lowell said, "I quite agree."

They headed back toward Meteor Crater.

On a hunch, Slocum brought them back across the site of their shoot-out with Culhane and his men earlier in the day.

"There's something I want to see first. We should have time . . ."

As Slocum had thought, the bodies of the two men that had been shot were nowhere to be found.

"Strange," Professor Lowell said.

"It sure is," Slocum said. "That's the same thing

that happened to the man who tried to get me in the crater."

He turned his horse toward Meteor Crater, and the professor, lost in thought, followed.

27

White Moon, chanting, led her Navajo brothers toward Meteor Crater.

The closer they got, the more uneasy Singing Arrow became. He looked at Kicking Horse and saw that he, too, felt uneasy.

Only Golden Eagle had a smirk on his face.

"More foolishness?" Golden Eagle asked.

"There's nothing foolish about this place," Kicking Horse said. "Our people have always heard . . . stories about it."

"You mean fairy tales, don't you?" Golden Eagle replied. He snorted. "Bedtime stories to scare children with."

Kicking Horse merely shrugged.

"And you?" Golden Eagle said, turning his sarcasm toward Singing Arrow. "Does our great chief believe in bedtime stories?"

Singing Arrow said nothing.

"Or does he only believe in *bed*," Golden Eagle persisted, looking toward White Moon.

As Golden Eagle and Singing Arrow moved to confront each other, White Moon said, "Look."

She pointed ahead of her, and her open eyes stared straight ahead.

"We are there," she said softly.

In the light of the overhead sun, at the rim of Meteor Crater, stood Myra Hendricks, her horse tied nearby, just pulling the tarp from the half-hidden wagon filled with Professor Lowell's instruments.

In a moment Golden Eagle, whooping, had run ahead to pull Myra away from the wagon. Flinging back the tarp himself, he looked inside.

"This is it!" he shouted, and whooped again. "This is the wagon we wanted!"

Singing Arrow moved beside him, with Kicking Horse close behind.

They began to pull boxes from the wagon, and then to slide the long, felt-covered tube of the telescope out.

"Please!" Myra begged. "Leave that alone!"

Golden Eagle turned to grin at her.

Singing Arrow, ignoring Myra, had soon pulled the tube out and unrolled it, as well as the tripod legs.

In a little while the pieces of the telescope lay exposed on the ground. Golden Eagle opened the eyepiece box and began to fiddle with the oculars, holding one up to his eye.

"Saw an eyeglass man in Tucson once," he said, squinting. "He had a bunch of junk like this."

"It's not junk!" Myra said. "Please!"

Kicking Horse, trying to set up the tripod but getting it wrong, stepped back and looked at Myra.

"All right," he said, "*you* put it together then."

Singing Arrow and Golden Eagle both stopped what they were doing to look at Myra.

"That's a good idea," Golden Eagle said.

Singing Arrow nodded, walked to Myra and took her arm.

"Do it," he snapped.

Myra hesitated.

Golden Eagle approached, drew his bowie knife and flashed it in front of her.

"All right. Just don't break any of it, please!" Myra said, and as the three men laughed, she bent down to pick up a piece they had neglected to attach to the tripod, and set to work assembling everything.

As Myra did this, Singing Arrow wandered to where White Moon sat, in a cleared spot away from the wagon, near the edge of the crater.

She was chanting softly, rocking back and forth, in front of a series of symbols.

"What are they?" Singing Arrow said, bending down to examine the pictograph of stones arranged on the ground.

White Moon abandoned her chant and looked at him, smiling.

"It is what we seek," she said.

"I don't understand."

"The breath between the worlds," she said.

"Did you do this?" he asked, pointing to the stones.

"No."

"Who did, then?"

She went back to her chant, holding her hands out over the arrangement of rocks, a smile of contentment on her face.

Shaking his head, Singing Arrow went back to the wagon.

Thirty minutes later, Myra Hendricks stood back and said, "There. That's that way all of it goes. But please—"

Golden Eagle pushed her aside and said, "We'll do whatever we want with it. It belongs to us."

"It doesn't!" Myra protested. "Professor Lowell—"

"Never heard of him," Golden Eagle laughed. He turned to grin at Kicking Horse. "How much you think this stuff is worth?"

Kicking Horse shrugged and looked at Singing Arrow, who nodded thoughtfully.

"A lot, I bet."

"But where will we sell it?" Kicking Horse said. "We can't get rid of it around here. They'll all know it came from this professor fellow."

Singing Arrow said, "We'll take it south, to Tucson, or down to Mexico."

"Mexico's probably best," Kicking Horse said. "You can get rid of anything down there."

"Or buy anything," Golden Eagle said, grinning. He had turned his attention to Myra and was looking her up and down.

"But why buy when you've already got, right?" he said.

"Hold on," Kicking Horse said as Golden Eagle took a step toward Myra.

"Why?" Golden Eagle said.

Kicking Horse hesitated.

Singing Arrow said, "Later."

Golden Eagle, smiling broadly, looked from Singing Arrow to Kicking Horse and then pulled his bowie.

"I say now."

Myra, pointing to the telescope, said, "I'm not sure if it works or not."

"What?" Golden Eagle said, and all three braves turned to face her.

"The instrument. I'm not sure if I put it together correctly."

"If it doesn't work, we can't sell it," Kicking Horse said.

Snorting, Golden Eagle slipped his bowie knife into its sheath and stalked to the telescope. He stared squinting into the large end holding the objective lens.

"I don't see anything."

"That's not where you look," Myra said.

Golden Eagle, angry, said, "I know that."

He viciously swiveled the tube around and peered into the other end, which is minus an eyepiece.

"I still don't see anything," he snapped.

Myra stepped forward, took one of the eyepieces from its case and held it out.

"Put this in, then look through it," she said.

Golden Eagle grabbed the eyepiece from her, tried to slide it in the wrong way, then put it in correctly. He stared into the ocular, still squinting.

"Everything's fuzzy."

"Turn the knob," Myra said. "To focus it."

Golden Eagle found the knob and turned it.

"Ah!" he said, then frowned as the image became fuzzy again. In a moment he had turned the knob the other way, slowly bringing the view into focus.

He shouted and jumped back.

"What is it?" Kicking Horse asked, stepping forward.

Golden Eagle stood rubbing his eyes.

"The rocks!" he said. "They're going to fall on me!"

Opening his eyes, he stared at the spot the telescope was pointed to and saw that it was an outcrop of rocks by the edge of Meteor Crater a quarter mile away.

Kicking Horse laughed.

"I don't think they're close enough to fall on you!"

Golden Eagle approached the eyepiece carefully and again looked in. He pulled back, gasping,
stared at the spot the instrument pointed to, then
looked gingerly through the eyepiece once more.

"Upside down!" he snorted.

Moving aside, he let Kicking Horse examine he
view. Kicking Horse also jumped back, then got
used to the view.

"The rocks are closer, but they look like they're
hanging from the sky!"

"That's because the telescope is made to look
at objects in space," Myra said. She still hoped
to get them so interested in the instrument that
she could make a break for one of the horses and
ride off.

Golden Eagle grabbed at the telescope tube
and turned it away from the view of the rocks
as Kicking Horse still looked through it.

"Hey!"

The tube now pointed at the sky.

"Give it back to me," Golden Eagle said.

He pulled his bowie knife and Kicking Horse
moved away.

Golden Eagle scanned the sky, and then zeroed
in on the sun. He swiveled the telescope tube
around until it was pointed at the daystar.

Despite her wish to get away, Myra found herself saying, "Don't look!"

Golden Eagle pulled back, just as he was about
to look into the eyepiece, and glared at her.

"Why?"

"You'll burn your eye! It will concentrate the light of the sun and blind you!"

"Bah!" Golden Eagle said.

But as he had taken his eye from the ocular, Kicking Horse, laughing, had taken his place and looked down into the eyepiece—

Kicking Horse screamed in pain as a fiery bolt of light shot into his retina. He pulled away from the ocular, falling to the ground, holding his eye.

Myra saw her chance, as Golden Eagle dropped his bowie knife and bent down to see to Kicking Horse.

Myra ran for her horse, tied up next to the wagon. She quickly unleashed it and pulled herself into the saddle.

As she turned to flee, she saw Golden Eagle and Singing Arrow reacting behind her.

"Get her!" Singing Arrow shouted.

"Go!" Myra shouted to the horse, kicking its flanks, and the horse galloped off.

Ahead the trail broke off in two directions. To the left it led down a steep slope into Meteor Crater.

Myra hesitated for a moment, her horse neighing at her indecision, and then she chose the right trail, which angled sharply away in the other direction.

In a moment she knew she had made a mistake. A rocky bed slowed her down to almost a walk as the horse complained at the stones in its way.

Ahead of her the trail smoothed out, and Myra desperately sought to push the horse over the rough ground. If she could make it to the other side of the rock spill, she would be able to escape to the long, sloping desert floor below. They would never be able to catch her.

"Come on, boy—come on," she urged, as the horse kicked and complained over the path it was being forced to negotiate.

But the going was too slow, and the smooth trail was still out of reach.

Then Myra knew it was too late.

In a moment Singing Arrow had raced ahead and around her, cutting off her path.

Behind her Golden Eagle cut off her retreat and trotted up beside her, grinning.

"That could have been me writhing on the ground back there," he said. He laughed. "Thank you!"

He took the reins from her and led her horse back to the wagon, laughing.

"Tonight," he said, "I'll see the stars—and you!"

28

Vern Culhane laughed grimly to himself.

Despite everything that had happend, he still could make his mission a success.

After all, there were only two things he had to accomplish, and both of them were still within his grasp.

The ore, and getting rid of Slocum.

Culhane patted the pocket where the mine map lay carefully folded. The Connors Mine held what he had come here for. By this time tomorrow, he would have it.

And Slocum would be dead.

Well, that was dicier, but he had no doubt he could take care of it.

And this time there would be no doubt.

Despite the loss of his three men, Vern Culhane found himself smiling.

Smiling at the thought of the death of John Slocum.

It was a pleasant thought, and he would look forward to making it reality.

After he did what he had to.

First things first.

Still smiling grimly, Vern Culhane turned his horse toward the Connors Mine.

29

As the sun began to fall in the west, Myra Hendricks knew she didn't have much time.

She knew the look on Golden Eagle's face—it was the same one she had seen on Vern Culhane's. What had been a pathetic attempt on Culhane's part would not be so easy to guard against with Golden Eagle—the Indian was powerful and, in his own way, just as dangerous as Culhane.

Myra guessed the young brave would make his move after dark.

By then she would have to be ready.

She couldn't help wondering what had happened to John Slocum and Professor Lowell. Logic had told her they would meet her back at the wagon. But now, after Kicking Horse's blinding, White Moon had ordered that everything be loaded back into the wagon and moved. Their new camp lay across Meteor Crater, and Myra could only hope that John Slocum would track them here.

In the meantime she watched Golden Eagle—who watched her.

And she formulated a plan . . .

• • •

As darkness fell it was not Golden Eagle but White Moon who came to her.

"Walk with me," the young Indian woman said to her and gently took her arm.

They went away from camp, under the dour look of Golden Eagle, and soon were alone. The stars were coming out, speckling the cool desert night. The entire Earth seemed quiet.

White Moon led Myra down into the bowl of the crater. As they descended, the night became even more still. They seemed to have entered another place, somewhere beyond the earth. There was a stillness in the air like a dream.

Near the bottom of the crater White Moon stopped and turned to face Myra.

"There are many tales my people tell," she said.

Myra said, "All peoples have their stories."

The slightest of smiles touched White Moon's lips.

"Some stories are true," she said.

Myra said nothing.

White Moon went on, "My people tell a story about the worlds in the sky, and the breath that moves between the worlds. It is, they say, the breath of the Maker. They say the Maker made Earth, but there was still much love in his heart left over, and so he made another world. But when he was halfway finished, the story says, he fell asleep, and didn't finish the world. It is a dry place, because the Maker fell asleep before he made the oceans. Only the water on the top and bottom of this world did he make, and that water is frozen in ice. But the rest of the world is dry desert."

White Moon regarded Myra with her huge, luminous eyes.

Myra said, "That's an interesting story."

"My people say that when the Maker woke up from his rest, it was already too late to remake this second world, because there were people living on it. So instead he blew his breath between the worlds, and said that the people from one world could visit the other. Many, many years ago, my people say, men and women from the dry world came to the Earth, and stayed." She spread her hands. "In fact, it is said that they landed in this very place, and that after their landing their great ship exploded in a ball of fire."

White Moon's huge eyes gazed at Myra unblinking.

"It is said that those men and women were the beginning of my people."

Myra said, softly, "That's a very beautiful story."

White Moon, the faint smile touching her lips again, said, "They also say the breath between worlds is still there, and that more people may come from the dry world to this one."

Now White Moon looked up away from Myra, and when Myra turned, she saw that the squaw was looking at the planet Mars, just rising above the desert horizon.

Myra silently put her hand on White Moon's arm.

"Are we sisters?" White Moon whispered.

Myra was about to open her mouth when she saw Golden Eagle standing behind the two of them, smirking.

"So, now I have my pick!" the brave laughed.

Myra saw Singing Arrow making his way quickly down the slope of the crater toward them.

"Golden Eagle—stop!" the young chief said.

Golden Eagle laughed, and as Singing Arrow reached them, Golden Eagle suddenly grabbed Myra by her arm and announced, "This squaw is mine! I claim her now!"

Instantly White Moon said, "No."

Singing Arrow joined White Moon and shook his head also.

"I say she is mine!" Golden Eagle demanded. Holding Myra's arm tightly, he began to force her to walk away from the others.

"You cannot," White Moon said simply.

"What do you say, *Chief*?" Golden Eagle spat. "Do you still side with your woman? You would not let me have White Moon—now you must let me have this squaw!"

"No," Singing Arrow said.

"Then I will take her after you die!"

Instantly Myra was thrown to the ground as Golden Eagle slid his bowie knife from its sheath to face Singing Arrow. The young chief drew a knife also.

The two braves circled each other, until Singing Arrow made the first attempted strike, missing in a wide arc.

In a second Golden Eagle, a tense grin on his face, had struck under the other's blow, cutting a swath up and across Singing Arrow's arm.

A line of blood burst forth.

"The great chief is bloodied!" Golden Eagle laughed.

Grimly Singing Arrow ignored the blood and tried again to strike.

Again his slashing arc was wide, and again Golden Eagle came underneath, this time barely missing Singing Arrow's abdomen.

Then Golden Eagle rushed, and the two braves locked arms and went down.

For a moment it looked as though Singing Arrow would best the other brave—but then the two figures rolled in the dust, and suddenly Golden Eagle was on top of his rival, his sharp blade trying to force its way down against Singing Arrow's straining guard.

"Wait!" Myra called out, seeing that Golden Eagle was about to win.

Two two combatants ignored her.

"There's treasure in the desert—something more valuable than the instruments in the wagon!"

The two men, holding their position, turned their attention to her.

"Stop fighting and I'll tell you," she said.

Golden Eagle suddenly stood up, and let Singing Arrow do the same.

"Well?" Golden Eagle spat.

"In the desert, not far from here, there is a mine. What it has in it is more valuable than gold."

"Where is this mine?" Golden Eagle demanded.

"It is called the Connors Mine," Myra said.

"The Connors mine!" Golden Eagle laughed. "It's been played out for years!"

"This treasure is something new," Myra persisted. "Something they didn't know was there, that wasn't needed until now."

Golden Eagle stared at her, weighing her words.

"It's possible," he said, finally. "They're always finding new uses for these rocks . . ."

"Go to the Connors Mine, and you will be wealthy," Myra said.

"What do you say, Chief?" Golden Eagle said to Singing Arrow. "Shall we believe the squaw, and be rich?"

Before Singing Arrow could answer, Golden Eagle had rushed toward him, plunging his bowie knife deep into the other man's chest.

Singing Arrow, a pained looked of surprise on his face, sank to his knees, then fell down into death.

Golden Eagle pushed the body with his foot, pulled the bowie knife out and shouted, "Now I am chief! And I say we will be rich!"

He wiped the blade on his side, sheathed it and then took a step toward Myra.

"And now you will be my squaw—"

From behind Golden Eagle, White Moon approached with a rock held aloft.

She brought it down on the brave's head.

Golden Eagle collapsed, and White Moon stood over him for a moment, the rock still held aloft in her two hands.

"I should kill him," she said fiercely, her huge, soft eyes filled with tears.

Instead she threw the rock aside and went to cradle the head of her dead chief, Singing Arrow.

"I wanted him to hear the breath between the worlds," she whispered.

After a moment she rose, looked down at the unconscious body of Golden Eagle and spat at it.

"We must go," she said, turning to Myra.

In another ten minutes they had taken two horses and left the camp behind. White Moon had thought of taking Kicking Horse with them, but the young brave was still asleep by the wagon, his eye swathed in bandages. He would only hold them up.

"He looked upon the breath of the Maker, and it almost killed him," White Moon whispered, and then they rode off.

Myra took the lead. There was only one thing to do, and that was find John Slocum and Professor Lowell, so she headed back to their original camp. She could only hope they would be there.

As they rode, and as Mars and the stars of Heaven wheeled overhead, White Moon began to chant, singing the songs of her people, and closed her eyes as she rode, nearly hiding the tears that flowed from them for what she left behind.

30

To Slocum's relief, one of the two figures riding toward them was Myra Hendricks.

It had been a grim ride back to Meteor Crater. The horses were tired, and had to be rested, and by the time they reached the original camp and found the wagon gone, hope had turned to true concern.

"I can't imagine what could have happened!" Professor Lowell said. To his great credit, he was much more worried about the loss of Myra than of his instruments.

"Posh!" he said. "I can replace everything in that wagon except Myra Hendricks!"

So they had set out, in the light of dusk, to find the wagon, and hopefully Myra Hendricks.

And now, halfway around the crater, they had found the more important half of what they sought.

As they rode closer, and Slocum made out the second figure—an Indian squaw—he pulled his Winchester and held it at the ready.

"John Slocum!" Myra waved. "Professor Lowell!"

In a moment they had pulled up beside the two women.

"Professor!" Myra smiled.

"Yes, I'm all right, my dear," Lowell said.

"John!"

Myra gave him a look of welcome that contained more than just thanks that he was safe.

"Where's the wagon?" Slocum asked.

Myra pointed back the way they had come.

"There was a fight. A fellow named Golden Eagle murdered another Indian. There are two of them left back there—"

Slocum was looking at the Indian squaw, who stared at him stonily and unblinking.

"This is White Moon," Myra explained.

"Those other two dangerous?"

Myra answered, "Golden Eagle is."

"Weapons?"

"They have knives. I didn't see any guns."

Myra turned to White Moon, who shook her head.

"Only knives. My people do not believe in the weapons of white men."

"That's fine with me," Slocum said. He spurred his Appaloosa. "I'll take care of this and be back."

"But Mr. Slocum—" Lowell said.

Slocum stopped and regarded the professor.

"Do you want your instruments back?"

"Why, yes—"

"Then wait here."

Slocum turned once more toward the other side of the crater and rode on.

Slocum had had more than enough of the whole business. Seeing Myra Hendricks again had only confirmed what he had thought before—when he was around her, he began not to think straight. It wasn't her charms—which he was glad enough to behold—but something else that he didn't want to mess with.

He was surprised, then, to see that she had caught up with him before he noticed her suddenly riding by his side.

"Aren't you glad to see me, John?"

"Where are the others?" Slocum snapped.

"Back where you told them to stay. I thought I should come with you."

Slocum looked straight ahead, rolled a quirly and lit it.

"Don't you like me anymore?" Myra asked.

"Liking's got nothing to do with it."

"You're afraid of me?" He knew she was smiling, but he refused to look at her.

"Not scared. Wary. You're like some kind of snake."

Now she laughed. "You really think I'm a snake?"

He looked around at her, threw his quirly to the ground.

"Not a snake then," he said sincerely. "But like something . . . different. A different kind of critter. And a man's smart to be careful around an animal he doesn't know."

She had sidled her horse up close to his, and now she put her hand on his leg.

"So now I'm an animal?" she cooed.

Slocum was suddenly all business.

"There's no time for that now," he said, riding ahead, peering into the faint night light.

Before long the wagon was straight ahead.

"Damn," Slocum said.

He said it not only for the scatter of broken instruments that lay on the ground. The professor's telescope looked as if it had been lifted and bashed against a rock; the tube was bent nearly double, and when Slocum dismounted, his boot crunched broken pieces of glass that had been in one of its eyepieces.

The rest of the equipment was in similar shape—even the small table had been broken to bits.

"Oh, my," Myra said. "Professor Lowell will be heartbroken."

"Damn," Slocum said again, for something that Myra didn't see. For there at the back of the wagon lay a figure spread out, feet dangling over the edge.

As Slocum got closer, he saw that the figure's throat had been cut. He had a bandage wrapped across one eye.

"Oh—" Myra gasped, and she clutched at Slocum not in passion but in shock.

"Who is he?"

"His name was Kicking Horse."

Behind them Slocum heard horses, and he turned to see the professor and White Moon riding slowly into the camp.

"Oh my, oh my," Lowell said, getting down from his horse to survey the damage.

White Moon rode up to the wagon and looked solemnly down at Kicking Horse.

"Golden Eagle has done this," she said.

"Will he come back?" Slocum asked.

"No," White Moon said. "He will seek the treasure that Myra told him of."

Slocum turned to Myra for explanation.

"It's something Vern Culhane was searching all those mines for. I told Golden Eagle about it to distract him, to try to get his mind off the things he was doing. But even if Golden Eagle finds it, it won't do him any good. It's worth more than gold—but only to Vern Culhane."

"What is it?"

She was mute—and again that feeling of strangeness washed over Slocum.

"Culhane's found it," she said simply. "In the Connors Mine."

"And?" Slocum asked, knowing she had more to say.

"And that's bad," Myra said.

"For whom?"

Myra's gaze was steady.

"For all of us."

31

To Slocum now, even with Myra Hendricks around, his mission was crystal clear.

"Anything you want from here, Professor?" he asked Lowell.

The scientist was picking around in the ruins, sighing over one piece of destroyed equipment after another. Finally he found something thrown in the brush and held it aloft, triumphant.

"Yes!" he said. "This is all I need!"

It was his sketchbook, and after that his spirits returned.

"Everything else can be replaced with money," he said. "But this is irreplaceable. My observations are more important to me than all the glass and metal in Arizona."

Slocum nodded.

"I'm glad. Because we're moving out now. We're going to ride all night, and into tomorrow. I want all of you back in Flagstaff by tomorrow afternoon."

Slocum looked at White Moon.

"You want to come?"

137

White Moon looked at Myra and said, "I will go where she goes."

"Fine," Slocum said.

"What are you going to do?" Myra asked.

"Plenty," Slocum said. "As soon as you're safe and out of the way."

Again she looked as if she had more to say, but she said nothing.

They rode out under the stars. But this time Slocum emptied his mind of all thoughts. It was like being back in the Confederate Army. He had a mission; he thought about his mission; he carried out his mission. No time for stray thoughts. That had been most true whenever his finger had been on the trigger of his rifle during a sharpshooting assignment. There was no need, and no gain, in thinking about the bluecoat officer in his sights. No gain in thinking of that officer as a man, or a father, or a husband, or a brother. Slocum had merely emptied his mind of all thought and let his trigger finger do the thinking.

It was not a way for a man to lead his whole life—but it was a useful tool to have when you needed it.

And the night tried to work on him. Again there were lights in the sky, and shooting meteors. The planet Mars rose red like a baleful eye and seemed to glare down at them.

"I've never seen a night of such activity," Professor Lowell said in wonder.

Slocum lit another quirly, ignored what was around him and looked straight ahead, leading his little band up the gentle slope that led, inevitably, to the foot of the San Francisco mountains and Flagstaff.

By the morning, the night seemed to have been a dream. Slocum, riding ever straight onward, felt as if he had been assaulted the entire night. Everything but demons had flown out at him, and by daybreak he wouldn't have been surprised to see Old Scratch himself standing in his path, laughing, throwing his head back and pointing at the sky for Slocum to look.

"I've never seen anything like it," Professor Lowell marveled, as dawn's first rays finally threw the stars back beyond the Earth and Mars's ruddy light faded into growing blue sky. "And I can't account for all those lights. There were three that I can vouch for as sporadic meteors, but those moving points of light, and those patterns they made . . ."

The scientist shook his head in wonder.

Welcoming the morning sun, Slocum brought himself out of his self-induced blankness and turned to Myra Hendricks.

"You have any explanation for what went on last night?"

"Why, no . . ."

But there was something more than disavowal on her face.

And White Moon looked at Myra with a knowing smile.

They climbed on. The ride was easy, and finally, before midday, they had left the purple sage and desert plain behind and reached the big-grained ponderosa pines that signaled their closeness to Flagstaff.

And then, almost too suddenly for Slocum, they were in the town, with people passing them in the wide street, with real shops under the sun—about as far away from the night as a man could get.

Professor Lowell was staring out over the far side of town.

"I seem to remember a very likely spot for my observatory, somewhere over that way. As soon as we get some rest . . ."

"I suggest you all get some rest," Slocum said.

"And you?" Myra said.

Slocum turned his horse around. "I'm heading back out. Rest is something I can get later."

"Why don't you sleep a couple of hours first?" Myra persisted.

He looked back at her evenly. "Because I want to do this work during the day—not at night."

Something flickered in the back of her fierce green eyes.

She said, "When you get back, I'll talk to you."

Slocum tipped his hat.

"I'll look forward to that talk—in more ways than one."

She almost smiled, but her face remained grim.

"Be careful, John Slocum. I'll tell you this about Vern Culhane. Right now he's the most dangerous man alive."

"I'll do what I have to."

"If you don't stop him . . ."

Slocum waited, but she would say no more. He tipped his hat again as he turned to White Moon.

"Tell me how to get to the Connors Mine," he said.

32

Slocum never got to the edge of town.

"You there!" someone called after him, and when Slocum turned, he saw a lawman on horseback closing in on him. The badge said, "Sheriff." In the distance, another lawman was camped near Myra, Professor Lowell and White Moon.

By old habit Slocum unhooked the thong covering his holster. The last thing he wanted was a fight, but if necessary, it was the first thing he'd look for.

He noticed, too, that this lawman had a rifle out, at the ready.

"Can I help you, Sheriff?" Slocum said when the man had pulled up alongside him.

"Sure can," the sheriff said, and he reached over to pull Slocum's Colt from its holster.

"The rifle, too, if you don't mind."

Slocum locked eyes with the man, and saw that the sheriff's face was just as hard as his own.

"You got laws in this town against carrying

firearms?" Slocum asked, reaching slowly down to pull the Winchester out of its scabbard.

The sheriff shook his head.

"No, mister, we don't. But we've got laws against murder."

Slocum handed the rifle over.

"Reckon you do, at that," Slocum said. He turned his horse around to follow the sheriff back to the center of town. "Let's clear this up."

Slocum was no stranger to misunderstandings, and since that's obviously what was going on here, he was willing to play along. There were always two choices in every situation, and in this one the wrong one would have been to make a play for his gun.

For one thing, Slocum knew, since the others were being held at casual gunpoint also, this had nothing to do with his past. There was always the chance that one of those old warrants that followed Slocum like some vague trail of ghosts had caught up with him. But that wasn't the case here. If it had been—well, gunplay would have been much more likely.

"Mind if I ask why all of us—including Professor Lowell here, who happens to be a well-known scientist—are being held?" Slocum asked when they had all been herded together.

The sheriff, a broad-faced man with a mustache under those hard eyes, seemed to relax a little now that they were all together. He pushed his hat back and said, "I think we'd be more comfortable talking inside the jail. Don't you think, Quint?"

His deputy, who Slocum figured was younger than he looked under his own mustache, a sparse imitations of his boss's, said, "Sure, Sheriff."

Quint waved his own rifle in the direction of the jail across the street.

"Shall we?" the sheriff said.

"Now just a minute," Lowell began, sitting straight up in his saddle. "I demand—"

"It's all right," Slocum said, holding his hand up to keep the professor from making their situation more difficult. "I'm sure the sheriff has a good reason for this." Slocum looked at the man evenly. "Mind at least giving us an idea?"

The sheriff motioned with his own rifle toward the jail, and smiled.

"No," he said.

There were two cells in the jail, and Quint and the sheriff put the women in one and the men in the other. Slocum figured it couldn't hurt to let Professor Lowell yell a little now, so he didn't stop the scientist's complaints. By now he had a few complaints of his own.

But he figured it was one of two things they were being held for, and before long he knew he was right.

The sheriff, whose name was Barnes, stood in front of them after they were locked in and said,

"I'm sorry to do things this way, but the way I see it, I don't have much choice."

He pushed his hat farther back and scratched his head.

"Actually, some damn strange things have been going on around here lately, and, well, I'm at the point I want some answers. A lot of people around here are getting nervous . . ."

He didn't seem to know how to proceed, but then he suddenly threw his hands up and looked at Lowell.

"Heck, Professor—I *know* you're a big shot and all, but since you got here, things have been just plain . . . *strange!*"

"How do you mean?" Lowell asked.

"Well . . . ," Barnes said. "People have been seeing all kinds of weird lights in the sky. And . . ."

With a sigh of frustration Barnes marched to his desk, pulled out a drawer and produced a magazine.

"One of the boys down at the livery stable got ahold of this," Barnes said. He opened it to a marked spot, where a drawing very much like one of Lowell's graced the page. Above it was the title, "Mars! Abode of Life?"

"You write this, Professor?" he asked Lowell.

"Yes, I did," Lowell said.

Barnes sighed again, then waved the magazine.

"Heck, I *know* it's just an article and all, but the people around here say you want to build

some kind of machine to get these here Martians
to come to earth!"

Lowell nearly laughed.

"That's not true at all! I merely want to build
a telescope—"

"I know, I know! But folks get things linked in
their heads, and now they think—bah."

He threw the magazine on the desk and turned
to face White Moon.

"Anyway, my other deputy was on his way
back from Winslow last night and found two of
your people dead, out by Meteor Crater. One of
them worked part-time over at the Western Union
office. Name was Flint. They'd both been knifed."
He turned to Lowell. "And all your . . . telescope
equipment was wrecked up nearby. My deputy
hightailed it back here, and from the way he
told it, you'd think he'd been attacked by those
peculiar lights and such all night long. When you
came into town, I was just about to gather a posse
and go looking for you. Feared the worst. But now
that you're here, and with all this other bizarre
business going on . . ."

Myra said, "White Moon and I know who killed
those two men. His name is Golden Eagle."

"That right?" Barnes said to White Moon.

At first White Moon said nothing, but then she
nodded.

Barnes said, "And where is this fellow Golden
Eagle?"

"Still in the desert," Myra said.

"Any idea where?"

Slocum waited to see if Myra would tell Barnes about the Connors Mine.

"No," Myra said.

"I see . . ."

Barnes scratched his head again. "Well, I'm sorry, but I'm afraid I'm going to have to hold you all here till I can raise some men and bring this Golden Eagle in. It's not that I don't believe you, it's just that . . . well, let's just say folks'd sleep better tonight if they know the professor here isn't out fooling around with the stars . . ."

Lowell sputtered, "That's the most preposterous—"

Barnes held up his hand.

"I know, Professor, I know. But it can't be helped."

"Do people in Flagstaff realize that if I situate my observatory here, it will bring a great deal of good to the area? Why, there will be many local jobs created, as well as a vast increase in tourism—"

Barnes was suddenly interested.

"Is that so?"

"Of course it's so!"

Barnes was scratching his head again. "Well, that might change things, in the long run. I'll have a talk with a few people. But I'm afraid that for now . . ."

Despite protests coming from the two jail cells, Barnes waved them off and left the jail.

"Well, it looks like we're here for the moment," Lowell said despondently.

"And," Myra said, looking over at Slocum, her face growing pale, "it looks like Vern Culhane may get what he came here for."

33

Golden Eagle was filled with a kind of power he had never known.

It wasn't just the killing that had filled him with this sense of omnipotence. The killings had been necessary—nothing more. He had almost regretted cutting Kicking Horse's throat—but after all, what else could he do? The brave would not have consented to come with him, and anyway, what good was he all but blind, anyway?

The death of Singing Arrow he regretted not at all. It had been coming for a long time. And for a long time Golden Eagle had known that it was he, not Singing Arrow, who should have been chief.

His only regret was that White Moon had escaped before he had made her his squaw, along with the other woman.

Well, there would be plenty of time for that later.

Now there was the matter of getting rich.

And all he had to do was find this "new gold."

The Connors Mine was not too far a ride. Golden Eagle figured he'd be there by sunset. Then he could sleep, and be ready to work the next morning.

And then—he would be rich.

Golden Eagle wondered how a rich Indian would be treated. He had never known one—but if what he thought would happen did, he would be treated like every other man with money. With respect. Even the white man respected money—it was the ticket into the white man's world. It was the ticket to do whatever he wanted.

Of course he would have to leave the Arizona Territory immediately. But that was no problem. With money, he could go anywhere and do anything he wanted. He had been to Wyoming, and once to Texas, but he didn't think he wanted to go to either of those places. One of the states to the east, perhaps—Missouri, or Illinois. Chicago— yes, that's where he would go. He had met an old man once, a member of his tribe, who had been to Chicago and said a man with money could be king there. The old man had come back with a vest from Chicago, which he wore all the time. Golden Eagle remembered wanting that vest.

Well, now he could have a hundred vests, if he wanted.

And women—yes, he would have all the women he wanted. White Moon was nothing compared to the women he would have.

Maybe he would even have white women!

Yes, that's what Golden Eagle wanted. He would have white women—a new one each night.

His money would buy him that.

And plenty more.

Anything he wanted.

With a whoop, Golden Eagle kicked his horse's flanks and headed, even faster, as the sun sank toward night, toward the Connors Mine and his waiting riches.

34

"John, you've got to do something," Myra whispered to Slocum.

In their adjoining cells they could see each other through the bars, even touch, but Myra was all business at the moment. She grabbed Slocum's arm, and Slocum could feel the tenseness in it.

"Just what is it you want me to do?" Slocum asked.

"I told you, if you don't stop Culhane, and soon . . ."

Slocum asked, "Why didn't you tell Sheriff Barnes about Culhane? Let him take care of it?"

Myra said, "Because he'd end up dead."

"What makes you think I won't end up dead, too?"

"I . . ." She turned away, and for the briefest moment he saw a tear on her cheek. When she looked back at him again, she said, "Don't ever say that again. The thought of it is just terrible."

"You really think I'm the only one who can take out Vern Culhane?"

"Yes," she said. "I think you're . . ."

Now she seemed to blush.

"What is it?" Slocum asked.

"I think you're the most wonderful man on Earth."

Slocum nearly laughed; he'd been called many things, but didn't ever recall being called that.

"The whole Earth?" he said, smiling.

"Yes," she said. "And we've got to get you out of here."

"Fine with me." Slocum shrugged.

The day dropped toward sunset. They were brought beans and bisquits, and Slocum and the others filled their bellies. Afterward, Slocum sat down in a corner with his hat over his eyes. Professor Lowell and, in the other cell, White Moon, lay down on single cots and soon were asleep.

Only Myra was fully awake, and Slocum watched from under the brim of his hat while she stood at her cell's high window, staring out for what seemed like forever, until darkness had nearly come. Red sunset streamed in through the small barred opening, and it was then that Slocum saw her pull a flat round brooch from her bosom and hold it up to the fading light.

Briefly Slocum saw red light bounce from the brooch as from a mirror, and angle up toward the sky.

"What the—" Slocum said, getting up, walking to the bars between the cells and holding them to see more clearly what Myra was up to.

"Shhhh," she said, without looking at him, and for the next few minutes she stood with the brooch in her hand, reflecting weak red sun in a kind of beam at the stars.

Then, suddenly, she repinned the brooch on her bosom and sat down on the floor.

"That's it," she said. "Now we'll see."

"See what?" Slocum asked.

The sheriff's deputy, Quint, yelled over at them, "Be quiet in there, you prisoners!"

Myra bowed her head and closed her eyes, and as Slocum watched her, she drifted off to sleep.

"We'll see . . . ," she whispered, and then she gently snored.

Slocum, shrugging, went back to his own spot, pulled his hat brim over his eyes and soon was snoring himself.

He didn't know how long he was asleep, but he was awakened loudly enough. He thought the world had caved in around him. There was a huge *whump*, and then the air was filled with dust.

Groping to his feet, Slocum checked the cell next to his and saw that the two women were all right. Choking with the dust now, he fought his way to the cot to find Professor Lowell sitting upright, coughing also.

"What in blazes—!" Lowell sputtered.

"John, you must get away!" Myra shouted.

"What?" Slocum said.

The deputy, Quint, was yelling at the front of the jail.

"The hole, John! Get out!"

Slocum now saw that the back of his cell was a shambles, with a hole where part of the wall used to be.

"But how—"

"Just go!" Myra shouted.

Ducking down, Slocum stepped through the hole and found himself in the outside world. Behind him there were shouts, and as Professor Lowell's startled face appeared in the hole, he was grabbed from behind by Quint.

"Go, Mr. Slocum!" Lowell shouted.

Without another word Slocum ran off.

To the side of the jail, as he had hoped, were their horses. His own Appaloosa looked to be in good shape.

"They feed you, boy?" he asked, and not waiting for an answer, he climbed on the animal's back, and a moment later, he was heading for the edge of town, leaving the noise and smoke behind.

It was only when he was well clear of Flagstaff that his mind began to work again. The city was behind him, and ahead of him lay the long slope down to the desert. There he would find Vern Culhane.

There, according to Myra, would be decided the fate of all of them.

And, Slocum now realized, he was heading into this with no weapon other than his brains—and, once again, he was at the mercy of the strange night.

35

Vern Culhane heard the sound far-off.

It sounded like a single rider.

Immediately he stopped his work. In the mine, by the light of his lantern, he had counted fifty-seven good-sized samples of the treasured ore before carting them out here to the shaft's opening.

Almost enough for what he needed.

But now there was other business to attend to.

A single rider meant it might be Slocum.

Vern Culhane wanted very much to deal with John Slocum now.

But almost immediately Culhane saw that it could not be Slocum after all. The man, whoever he was, was much too clumsy. He was riding out in the open, with no weapon in sight. He rode as if he were going to a picnic.

And now that the man drew closer, Culhane heard him laughing to himself.

"Gold!" the figure shouted into the night. "Better than gold! I'm gonna be rich!"

With a cruel smile, Culhane pulled himself into the shadows of night.

The man, whoever he was, had been misinformed.

But then, as Culhane waited in the rocks at the entrance to the mine, something strange happened.

The man disappeared.

"What in hell," Culhane muttered.

Immediately, Culhane tensed. He took his rifle from its spot, nestled between two rocks, and climbed up a short ledge over the entrance. There was the man's horse, and Culhane lowered the rifle, aiming it—

The horse was there, but the rider was gone.

Now Culhane's senses sharpened. He went into a kind of animal state of mind, cruel and cold, thinking with his instincts instead of his mind.

He realized what had happened.

The wind, what little there was of it, was behind him. It had been moving in the direction of the rider, who must have smelled him.

So whoever it was was good after all.

A worthy opponent.

The night, except for the rider's horse, which clopped by Culhane, was utterly silent.

"Damn it," Culhane muttered, "where are you?"

"Right here!" a voice, frighteningly close, called, laughing.

With lightning speed, Vern Culhane whipped around, his rifle hitting away the figure, who had nearly been upon him. Instantly Culhane realized what had happened—the man *had* still been on the horse, only hidden behind it. It had been a trick, a brilliant trick.

"Indian," Culhane spat out, half in admiration.

"Of course!" his opponent laughed, scrabbling away from the blow of the rifle, back into the dark.

Once more the night was silent.

Culhane, more alive than he had ever been in this place, crouched and waited.

And then he heard the Indian's voice, seemingly from far away to the left.

"Hey, cowboy—how come you're digging my treasure?"

Culhane was silent, but he crouched lower, his rifle ready, sweeping the area in front of the mine.

"Hey, cowboy," the voice came again, now from the *other* side, far away to the right.

"Hey, cowboy!" the voice said, right overhead.

Culhane looked up to see the Indian looming above him.

The figure jumped down upon him as Culhane raised his rifle.

"Get away from my treasure, cowboy!" the Indian yelled, laughing. "Golden Eagle says get away!"

Again Culhane hit at the figure with the barrel of his rifle, and once again the Indian scooted off into the night, hooting.

Angry now, Culhane ran after, and then suddenly stopped.

No, he thought. That's what he wants.

Culhane pulled back into the recesses of the rocks.

A line of cruel laughter broke from him, but he kept his voice low.

Enough of this, he thought.

"Hey, Golden Eagle!" he shouted out into the night.

He was met by silence, but he knew the Indian was listening.

"Hey, Golden Eagle, I'll tell you what! I'll split the treasure with you! Fifty-fifty!"

Again there was silence, but Vern Culhane could feel, could taste with his instinct, the Indian listening to him.

"Golden Eagle, are you listening? Hell, I'll even *give* you your half now! I've already dug it up!"

Now there was the briefest heightening of silence, as if the Indian could taste Culhane's words.

"Golden Eagle, you hear me?" He tried to sound defeated, scared, sick of battle. "Hell, I'll even give you something else! I'll let you have this magic talisman I found in the mine, next to the treasure!"

Culhane let four heartbeats go by, letting the Indian think about what he had just said.

"Here it is—come and get it!"

Culhane fished an oval piece of metal from his pocket and rubbed it with his thumb. Then he tossed it out onto the desert floor. It was glowing softly.

"Look what it can do, Golden Eagle! It makes the stars move!"

Above, lights appeared out of the heavens and moved around.

"Just pick it up and they'll move for you!"

Now came the payoff.

Culhane knew the Indian would go for the oval piece of metal. And when Golden Eagle appeared out of the shadows to pick it up, Culhane already was aiming his rifle, and he put a bullet deep into the Indian's knee.

Golden Eagle shouted in pain, grabbed for his knee even as his other hand reached for the talisman, just out of his reach.

Culhane strode out to stand over Golden Eagle, who now gave up reaching for the talisman and instead drew a bowie knife from a sheath at his side. Though his face was contorted with pain, he held the knife up menacingly toward Culhane.

"That—treasure—is—mine," Golden Eagle spat out, teeth clenched.

"I don't think so," Culhane said coldly.

He kicked the bowie knife out of the Indian's hand, then bent down to pick up the talisman and put it back in his pocket.

"In fact, this is mine, too."

Drawing back his boot, Culhane kicked Golden Eagle in his wounded leg.

Across the desert cries of pain echoed.

And echoed for some time, before ceasing.

36

By the time Sheriff Barnes's other deputy, Ackers, had reached the jail on a run, Barnes had things pretty much under control.

Barnes put Professor Lowell in the jail cell with White Moon and Myra Hendricks and stood scratching his head with his hat pushed back as he regarded the large hole in the other cell.

"Darndest thing I've ever seen," he said. He turned to Lowell with something like admiration on his face.

"How'd you do it? Dynamite?"

Lowell shook his head.

"I have no idea what happened, Sheriff."

Barnes sighed.

"Right."

The sheriff turned to Ackers, who if anything looked even younger than Quint, and said, "You stay here with them. With your rifle cocked and ready. Anything like that happens," he said, pointing to the hole in the jail cell, "and you have my permission to start shooting at anything and everything."

"Sheriff Barnes?" Lowell said.

"Yes?" the sheriff answered.

"Sheriff, I want to be completely honest with you. I have no idea what happened here. But I do know that much of the trouble in this area has been caused by a man named Vern Culhane. He and two of his henchmen have been trying to kill Mr. Slocum, and us as well."

Barnes said, "Why didn't you tell me this before?"

Lowell hesitated, looked at Myra and then answered.

"Because Miss Hendricks here considers this Culhane to be extremely dangerous. She believes that Mr. Slocum can handle him, but that no one else can."

Barnes looked at Lowell with disbelief and then turned to his two deputies.

"Hear that, boys?" he said. "Slocum without a gun can handle this character, but we can't!"

The three of them began to laugh.

Lowell, without smiling, said, "You will be able to find this fellow somewhere around the Connors Mine."

Barnes stopped laughing and said, "Well, thank you, Professor, for that information. And we'll do what we can to rein this Culhane in. If the story checks out, I guess that would be the ticket out of this mess for you and the two ladies there."

He walked out, Quint in tow, still scratching his head.

"Darndest thing I've ever seen . . ."

• • •

With five men behind him, Sheriff Barnes was on his way down into the desert plains as night fell. Barnes knew the area like the back of his hand.

"Figure this Culhane is as dangerous as that professor says?" Quint asked, a little nervously.

"No man's as dangerous as other men think," Barnes said. "I've been working this area for twenty years, and I've seen plenty of so-called desperadoes ride through. Most of them were tired and scared and sick of running. A few were desperate."

He patted his Winchester rifle.

"Most of them didn't like the sight of one of these at all."

Quint was silent as they rode on, but he silently slipped his own rifle out of its scabbard and made sure it was loaded and ready to fire.

Back in Flagstaff, in the jail, Ackers, the young deputy, looked at Professor Lowell with goggle eyes for a while before opening his mouth. He had read the magazine article, looked at the rotogravure picture of the Martian surface, listened to all the stories around town. He had found the two Indian bodies in the desert and seen strange lights in the sky.

Finally he worked up his courage to speak.

"Hey, Perfessor," he said.

Lowell looked up and said, "Yes?"

"You really think them Mars folk is gonna land? I mean, right here?"

Wearily, Lowell shook his head.

"No, son, I don't."

"But if they do, you think they's got big fish eyes and such, and long straggly arms and legs, from marching around on that red Martian dirt?"

Patiently Lowell said, "That's not quite what I said in my article, young man."

Still goggle-eyed, Ackers ignored Lowell's answer.

"Gosh," he said, "I hope they don't take my daddy's ranch or nothing." He looked at Lowell again, if anything his eyes goggling out even more.

"You think they want our womenfolk?"

Lowell threw up his hands, a trace of anger held in check.

"Young man," he said evenly, "I did not write, in that magazine article or anywhere, that Martians were going to invade Earth, now or ever. Nor did I imply in any of my writings that they had fish eyes, or any such thing, or, especially, that they were longing to invade Earth in order to take our female population away from us. Now *please* stop asking foolish questions and stop worrying!"

Completely ignoring what Lowell had said, the young man turned back to the magazine article, studied the rotogravure picture again with his bugged-out eyes and said, "Gosh . . ."

Lowell turned to Myra in exasperation and noted the continuing look of disapproval on her face.

"Myra, dear," Lowell said, "I hope you understand that I *had* to tell Sheriff Barnes the truth. It was not fair to him, or to Mr. Slocum."

Her eyes softened, and she said, "I understand, Professor."

"Good," Lowell said. "After all, Mr. Slocum is alone, and this Vern Culhane is a very dangerous character."

"More dangerous than you'll ever know, Professor."

"And if, as you believe, Mr. Slocum is the only one who can stop him, there's still a chance he might do that, isn't there? He did have a head start, after all."

"You may be right, Professor."

"You do understand why I had to tell Sheriff Barnes those things, don't you?"

"Yes, I do, Professor," Myra Hendricks said, putting her hand briefly on the scientist's arm.

"But I hope you understand," Myra continued wearily, turning to look out the small window of their cell into the night sky, "that you may have, without at all wishing it, condemned all those men, John Slocum included, to death.

"And," she continued, in a whisper only she could hear, "this world also."

37

Now, at last, Slocum knew that the showdown with Vern Culhane was coming.

He could feel it in his bones. The night, the dangerous night, whispered it to him, and the very air was charged with danger and the scent of confrontation.

The lack of a weapon didn't concern him at this point. He wasn't a fool; he would have been much more content with his Colt in his cross-draw holster and his Winchester nestled and ready in his saddle scabbard, right behind his knee. If he had been heading toward a gambling game when he got into this mess, he would have at least had his Remington .41 derringer in its cuff holster. Those two deadly barrels could do a lot of damage.

But Slocum had the best weapon of all—his mind. And Vern Culhane's weakness was that he wanted Slocum so badly—and might make a bad slip to get him.

There was a plan of sorts in Slocum's head, and it just might work. It counted on Culhane being so busy with his mining activities that he didn't hear a quiet man coming up on him . . .

• • •

And there, hours before dawn, in the light of a
nearly full moon and the Milky Way, under the
baleful eye of Mars in the sky, sat the Connors
Mine nestled on a flat plain before him.

Slocum tied his Appaloosa a good half mile away
and set out on foot. Quiet as a Comanche he made
his way forward.

Almost immediately he knew that someone, and
not Vern Culhane, had come this way before him.
His senses sharpened, he soon found his evidence:
deep, sloppy horse tracks in the desert floor.

Silently Slocum followed them.

A hundred yards from the mine opening, he
turned all but invisible. Fifty yards in he saw
that something had happened. The horse prints
turned suddenly into a riot of steps. The rider had
been brought up short here. Then the prints took
off in a different gait straight for the entrance to
the mine.

And Slocum heard no sound at all. If there was
a man in that mine, he was being as quiet inside
as Slocum was outside.

Stealthily, ready for anything, Slocum approached the opening.

At the mine he had his answer. Culhane had
been and gone. Near the opening was a smoothed-
out area where a good amount of something had
been stacked. Nearby were the prints of two
horses, one of them the one whose prints Slocum
had followed up to the mine. They led north into

the desert, and Slocum could see that they had been weighted when they left.

And there on a stick at the mine shaft's opening was a calling card for Slocum: an Indian's head, cut off raggedly at the neck line, the mouth open in a silent scream.

Slocum imagined it was Golden Eagle, come to collect his treasure.

The inside of the mine shaft was empty.

Vern Culhane was gone.

As Slocum stepped back outside, a dance of sudden lights began in the sky overhead, circling the planet Mars and seeming to draw closer to the Earth.

A prickle of something like dread crawled up Slocum's back.

And then he heard, not very far off, the sound of gunshots in the night, and the shouts of men, and the boom of the cruel laughter of one in particular, which seemed to mock everything on the ground and in the sky.

"I've had enough of Verne Culhane," Slocum spat.

And then, gut tightening with the certainty that if he didn't hurry all would be lost, Slocum was running, calling his Appaloosa to him and then climbing expertly onto its smooth back, settling into his saddle and kicking the fluid beast, telling it to run, run north like it had never run before.

38

Already two of Barnes's men, including Quint, were dead, and another wounded.

To Barnes, the attack seemed to come out of thin air. One minute they were making their way down into a shallow valley in the desert floor, and the next moment the night was alive with gunfire, and that valley had been turned into a killing zone.

Quint was the first to go down, shot straight through the heart, and then Fred Graham, the town blacksmith, had followed. All of a sudden none of them knew where to run to, what to do.

"Get down!" Barnes shouted, thinking back on his days in the Confederate Army. "Get down behind your mounts and locate that gunfire!"

While he was shouting all this, another of his men was hit, but soon the three of them remaining alive were at least down on the ground behind some reasonable kind of cover.

At least Barnes thought so. But after a lull in the shooting, during which Barnes and the other man readied their rifles, fire erupted out from behind them, where they had just come from!

"Dammit! How many of them are there?" Barnes shouted.

In answer there was laughter from above.

"Just enough to kill you all!" a cruel voice shouted down at them.

The night exploded with more shots, those from above and those from within the killing zone. Barnes's horse was shot dead in front of him.

The laughing voice, now sounding farther away, said, "I've got something to do! I'll be back for you later!"

Suddenly there was quiet again from above, and Barnes put his hand on the man next to him to quiet his fire.

"Think it's over?" the man said in some panic, staring into Barnes's face with wide eyes in the moonlight.

"No, I don't."

But the silence stretched.

Then there was a sound from above them, where the original shots had come from.

Barnes raised his rifle to fire.

"Hold it!" a voice shouted. "It's me, John Slocum! Culhane's moved off!"

"Hold your rifle on him," Barnes ordered, and then as Slocum made his way down into the bowl, Barnes stood up.

"Don't know if I'm glad to see you or not, Slocum."

"Arrest me, then, Sheriff," Slocum shot back,

"or give me a rifle, because I saw where Culhane went."

"I'll come with you—" Barnes began.

"No," Slocum said. He pointed to the sheriff's mounts. "Culhane killed all the horses. Figured he'd come back for you when he felt like it. It's me he wants."

"Then let me go after him—" Barnes tried.

"It's me or nobody."

Barnes stared up at Slocum, his face hard in the moonlight, and then said to the wide-eyed man next to him, "Give him your rifle, Curly."

"But—"

"Give it to him, dammit."

Slocum nodded thanks as the rifle was handed up to him.

"I'll take care of it, Sheriff."

"I hope so," Barnes said. "Or I swear I'll take care of you."

Slocum galloped off, up the slope and away, as Barnes turned to his wounded and dead.

A fair fight now, that's what Slocum had.

And that's all that any man could ask, wasn't it? A fair fight?

Culhane, though, wouldn't play fair.

But Slocum had an idea that Culhane didn't have time to think about it one way or another. For ahead of him, on the high desert plain, Slocum could see his opponent loaded down with two horses bearing ore.

Which meant that he had an appointment to keep.

When he was barely in rifle range, Slocum raised his weapon and fired a shot over Culhane's head to slow him down.

"I told you I'd be back for you, didn't I?" Culhane's cruel laughter called back. He kept going. "Got someplace to be! Plenty of time for you to die later!"

Again the cruel laughter, and no break in the pace of Culhane's horses.

"It's me!" Slocum called out, firing another shot toward his opponent. "It's John Slocum!"

Instantly Culhane stopped in his tracks. Even from that distance Slocum could almost taste the other man's hate.

But then, as in an optical illusion, Culhane's loaded horses were there, but the man was gone.

Slipped away into the night.

Slocum quickly slid down from his saddle and moved off to the right.

A fair fight, and he would keep it that way.

Slocum turned all but invisible.

Trouble was, so had Culhane. For as hard as he tried, Slocum heard nothing, saw nothing. The silvery illuminated desert floor before him was all but empty.

And then came the slightest of sounds, just as a shot nearby knocked Slocum's rifle from his hands, and he heard someone rush at him in the night—

And then Culhane had him. The man threw his own rifle aside and had Slocum in his grip, the tight grip of a monster, and the hate in his voice was close by Slocum's ear:

"I'm gonna kill you slow, Slocum. Gonna break each bone in your body and let you feel it."

With the mightiest of efforts, knowing that he would only get one try, Slocum threw a hand behind him, grabbing at Culhane's head, pulling the man's tightly knotted bandanna down over his face to his neck and then twisting . . .

Culhane kept his grip on Slocum even as he fought for breath.

"Gonna . . . kill you . . . Slocum . . ."

Slocum twisted the bandanna tighter, completely blocking the other man's wind.

"Gonna—"

Suddenly desperate, Culhane loosened his grip and raked at Slocum's face, his body, punching him, grabbing at Slocum's neck and suddenly finding purchase again.

Slocum began to fight for air, and now it was a race as Slocum's own wind was cut off and suffocation came near—

But then Culhane's grip weakened, and his hands fell away, and Slocum saw the man's wide eyes as he fought for a last breath that would never come. Slocum kept the pressure on as Culhane fell to his knees, then slumped over into death.

"That's what you meant for me originally,

wasn't it, Culhane?" Slocum said, catching his own breath.

Then he looked up into the suddenly lightening sky, knowing there was something else he must do, and left Culhane's body, He approached the horses, each of which was laden with packs of ore.

One by one Slocum removed most of the packs and scattered them across a wide area. Then he smacked the horses to make them run, with part of the ore still on their backs, never to be gathered into one spot.

Far off, in the direction Culhane had been heading, Slocum saw a light in the sky that grew suddenly bright, as if searching, and then grew dim again, receding into the sky.

Weary, spent, Slocum gathered the rifle Barnes had given him, mounted his Appaloosa and rode off to find the sheriff and his men.

When he looked behind him, he saw that light again, getting brighter and then fading, and he knew that if he went back, he would probably find Vern Culhane's body gone.

The sun rose, a welcome sight.

Once again it was day, and the strange, unknowable night was gone.

Slocum rode on.

When he reached Barnes and his surviving men, still nestled and ready among their dead horses, he handed Barnes the rifle back, stock first, and said simply, "It's over."

39

And so, hours later, after a weary little band had made its way back to Flagstaff, it was truly ended.

Barnes completely cleared Slocum and the others. When the professor was freed, he approached Slocum excitedly and said, "I've found the spot for my observatory! Young Ackers here," he said, turning to the goggly-eyed deputy, "knows someone with the perfect site, within the limits of Flagstaff! I can begin work as soon as possible!"

"That's good, Professor," Slocum said.

Lowell shook Slocum's hand vigorously and pressed seventy-five dollars in gold coin into his palm, as well as a box of Havanas.

"I can't thank you enough, Mr. Slocum! My dream will come true, and you helped it happen!" He looked closely into Slocum's face. "You *will* come to look at Mars through my telescope, when work is completed?"

"I'd be honored," Slocum said.

"Good!"

Lowell nearly ran off, with Ackers in tow, in the direction of his promised site.

And then suddenly Myra Hendricks was at Slocum's side, smiling.

"You *are* the most wonderful man on Earth," she said.

"And what happens to you now?" Slocum asked.

"I told Professor Lowell I'd be going back to Boston."

"Will you?"

"I *will* be going back . . . home," she said. She moved closer to him, and her fierce green eyes looked hungrily up at Slocum. "But not before I see you again."

"Hey, Sheriff!" Slocum called to Barnes. "There a good place where a man can rent a room in this town?"

And then they were in each other's arms again— this time in the daylight.

But Myra was no less a tiger with the sun up. Slocum had thought that a part of her hunger was fed by the night, but he was wrong. If anything she was hungrier by day, and more beautiful.

Again Slocum marveled at her perfect body. Even as the door was closed on their room, she was out of her clothes and into Slocum's arms. Laughing, she pulled him down onto the bed, then straddled him, feeling him stiffen beneath her.

Then suddenly she enclosed him, pulling him deep inside.

"Oh, John, yes!"

She arched her back, bringing her perfect breasts before his mouth, where he tasted them, one and then the other. Her nipples hardened to buttons, and he ran his tongue around them before biting softly.

"Oh, John!" she screamed. "Where I come from no man can do this!"

And indeed he was straight and hard and long inside her. She moved on him like a machine, oiled and primed, riding him like a fine horse, tightening like a spring for what seemed like hours and might have been, until Slocum saw her eyes glaze as her mouth opened in ecstacy--

"John, *now!*"

Slocum obliged, letting his white river burst out of himself into her, and she seemed to rise on the tide, filled and expanded, her love channel suddenly rocking like an exploding mechanism as she writhed above him, holding on tight and screeching with each break of the waves—

"Oh! Oh! Oh!"

With the peak of her orgasm, Slocum let one final spurt blast into her, and she literally rose off him, her open space leaving his tip, dripping both her juice and his as she screamed out in pleasure before dropping down onto him again, taking one final deep thrust from his rock-hard love weapon.

She fell onto his chest, spent, heaving for breath, done and happy.

"John . . . ," she panted. "I can't tell you . . ."

He smiled up at her.

"Best in the world?"

"In *all* worlds . . . ," she said, and suddenly she laughed.

And then they were finished, and she told him a story.

"Let's call this make-believe," Myra said. "Let's say a long time ago visitors came to Earth from a red planet in the sky and were stranded here. This was long before the Arizona Territory existed. And eventually these visitors made themselves at home, and all but forgot about their cousins in the sky, except in legends where they talked about 'the breath between the worlds.'

"And then a time came where there was much upheaval on the red planet. Two factions, both powerful, began to quarrel. One was evil and devised a plan to visit Earth again, only this time to conquer it. For Earth had a valuable mineral in very short supply on the red planet, which would make it possible for *many* ships to come with many warriors.

"The other faction opposed this and said the only reason to visit Earth would be to give greetings to our brothers and sisters who were lost here so long ago.

"Both factions were powerful, and when the evil faction seized most of the valuable mineral left on the red planet to fuel a spaceship, and sent a band of desperadoes to Earth to find the valuable mineral to make invasion possible, the other faction knew it had to act, for the sake of both planets.

"So their princess was sent in another ship using the rest of this rare mineral, to stop the bad faction and, if possible, to find the long lost visitors. Only her ship had been sabotaged, and it landed near Boston, not the Arizona Territory, where she needed to be. She had a small amount of power and a few gadgets to help her. She made pictographs in the desert to signal her ship and could make limited use of lights in the sky, small devices from her ship which she could signal directly. But mostly she had to use her wits and hooked up with a brilliant earth man interested in the red planet and on his way to Arizona . . ."

Myra put her hand on Slocum's shoulder.

"And the princess found a wonderful man to help her . . ."

She smiled, and after a while Slocum smiled, too.

"Nice story," he said.

Myra nodded.

"Think anybody'd believe it?"

Myra shrugged. "Actually, I told a little of it to a man named Burroughs on the train out to Arizona, and *he* thought there was something to it."

"Must've been a fool," Slocum said.

Myra nodded and smiled.

"And now?" Slocum said.

"Now I go back to . . . Boston, and White Moon is coming with me."

"You mean she's—"

"That was just a story, John. But if it were true, White Moon would be one of the lost visitors from the red planet."

"I see."

Myra's green eyes flashed.

"But before I go," she said, pushing him onto his back and straddling him again, "story time is over."

It was, and John Slocum obliged.

Later, when Slocum was dozing, or perhaps dreaming, he felt Myra Hendricks leave the bed and whisper into his ear:

"Good-bye, John Slocum, best man of all worlds . . ."

Slocum smiled in his sleep.

40

When Slocum was ready to ride again, it was nighttime.

Cursing under his breath, but at the same time smiling as if he felt this was somehow only right, he mounted his Appaloosa and turned it out of Flagstaff.

Where would he go?

He had no idea. For suddenly he had a full poke and a box of Havanas, and he didn't feel in a rush to go anywhere in particular. Let the desert wind take him where it would.

Or the breath between the worlds.

He laughed, and pulled a fresh, sweet Havana from his pocket and fired it up. The tobacco was like a woman's kiss on his lips.

A woman from . . . Boston.

Slocum laughed again, and looked at the sky, and nearly ran over something in the dark.

"Good heavens!" a voice called out. "Why, is that you, Mr. Slocum? I believe I smell a Havana!"

Slocum looked down to see Professor Lowell standing there with his sketchbook, his partially destroyed but still usable telescope mounted on its now rickety tripod.

"Hello, Professor," Slocum said amiably.

Lowell, smiling broadly, spread his arms around him.

"Well, what do you think? Isn't it the ideal spot for my observatory?"

Slocum surveyed the area around them—flat and wide, with the sky a beautiful clear bowl above them. In the soft distance ponderosa pines nestled the low horizon.

"I'd say it's perfect," Slocum said.

Lowell sighed like a contented new father.

"It will be magnificent! And the seeing is . . . just perfect!" He patted his telescope. "And that young man Ackers was kind enough to retrieve my Alvan Clark refractor for me! It took a bit of work to realign the objective, but it's more than usable!"

"I'm happy for you," Slocum said.

Lowell suddenly looked up, to where the reddish eye of Mars was rising.

"Look, Mr. Slocum!"

A single light, bright in the sky, suddenly shot up and then dwindled to a stellar dot.

Slocum nodded.

"Got a feeling that's the last of those you'll see, Professor."

Lowell grunted. "But soon, I'll study Mars to my heart's content, right here from this spot! If only Myra had stayed to study it with me!"

"I have a feeling she'll be seeing even more of it than you, Professor," Slocum said.

But Lowell hadn't heard him and was already back at his dented eyepiece, sketchbook in hand.

"Good-bye, Professor," Slocum said, moving off.

"Good-bye, Mr. Slocum!" Lowell called out, without looking up. "And remember, come back to look through my new instrument!"

"I'll try to do that," Slocum said.

And in a moment he had left the excited scientist behind and was once more alone in the night.

The night which strangely didn't seem so hostile anymore, or strange.

And suddenly Slocum did not feel so alone at all.

He looked up and saw the red eye of Mars shining down upon him warmly, and, he could have sworn, even without whiskey in him, that it winked.

If you enjoyed this book, subscribe now and get...

TWO FREE

A $7.00 VALUE—

If you would like to read more of the very best, most exciting, adventurous, action-packed Westerns being published today, you'll want to subscribe to True Value's Western Home Subscription Service.

Each month the editors of True Value will select the 6 very best Westerns from America's leading publishers for special readers like you. You'll be able to preview these new titles as soon as they are published, *FREE* for ten days with no obligation!

TWO FREE BOOKS

When you subscribe, we'll send you your first month's shipment of the newest and best 6 Westerns for you to preview. With your first shipment, two of these books will be yours as our introductory gift to you absolutely *FREE* (a $7.00 value), regardless of what you decide to do. If

you like them, as much as we think you will, keep all six books but pay for just 4 at the low subscriber rate of just $2.75 each. If you decide to return them, keep 2 of the titles as our gift. No obligation.

Special Subscriber Savings

When you become a True Value subscriber you'll save money several ways. First, all regular monthly selections will be billed at the low subscriber price of just $2.75 each. That's at least a savings of $4.50 each month below the publishers price. Second, there is never any shipping, handling or other hidden charges—*Free home delivery*. What's more there is no minimum number of books you must buy, you may return any selection for full credit and you can cancel your subscription at any time. A TRUE VALUE!

A special offer for people who enjoy reading the best Westerns published today.

WESTERNS!

NO OBLIGATION

Mail the coupon below

To start your subscription and receive 2 FREE WESTERNS, fill out the coupon below and mail it today. We'll send your first shipment which includes 2 FREE BOOKS as soon as we receive it.

Mail To: **True Value Home Subscription Services, Inc. P.O. Box 5235 120 Brighton Road, Clifton, New Jersey 07015-5235**

YES! I want to start reviewing the very best Westerns being published today. Send me my first shipment of 6 Westerns for me to preview FREE for 10 days. If I decide to keep them, I'll pay for just 4 of the books at the low subscriber price of $2.75 each; a total $11.00 (a $21.00 value). Then each month I'll receive the 6 newest and best Westerns to preview Free for 10 days. If I'm not satisfied I may return them within 10 days and owe nothing. Otherwise I'll be billed at the special low subscriber rate of $2.75 each; a total of $16.50 (at least a $21.00 value) and save $4.50 off the publishers price. There are never any shipping, handling or other hidden charges. I understand I am under no obligation to purchase any number of books and I can cancel my subscription at any time, no questions asked. In any case the 2 FREE books are mine to keep.

Name _____

Street Address _____ Apt. No _____

City _____ State _____ Zip Code _____

Telephone _____

Signature _____
(if under 18 parent or guardian must sign)

Terms and prices subject to change. Orders subject
to acceptance by True Value Home Subscription
Services, Inc.

14182-9